A Ranger for Christmas

Stella Bagwell

HARLEQUIN® SPECIAL EDITION

Recycling programs
for this product may
not exist in your area.

ISBN-13: 978-1-335-46616-7

A Ranger for Christmas

Copyright © 2018 by Stella Bagwell

Printed in U.S.A.

After writing more than eighty books for Harlequin, **Stella Bagwell** still finds it exciting to create new stories and bring her characters to life. She loves all things Western and has been married to her own real cowboy for forty-four years. Living on the south Texas coast, she also enjoys being outdoors and helping her husband care for the horses, cats and dog that call their small ranch home. The couple has one son, who teaches high school mathematics and is also an athletic director. Stella loves hearing from readers. They can contact her at stellabagwell@gmail.com.

Books by Stella Bagwell

Harlequin Special Edition

Men of the West

Her Man on Three Rivers Ranch
The Arizona Lawman
Her Kind of Doctor
The Cowboy's Christmas Lullaby
His Badge, Her Baby...Their Family?
Her Rugged Rancher
Christmas on the Silver Horn Ranch
Daddy Wore Spurs
The Lawman's Noelle

Montana Mavericks: The Lonelyhearts Ranch

The Little Maverick Matchmaker

Montana Mavericks: The Great Family Roundup

The Maverick's Bride-to-Order

Visit the Author Profile page
at Harlequin.com for more titles.

With much love to my brother, Charles Cook,
and my sister-in-law, Denise Cook.

Chapter One

"How many times do I have to tell you, Mort? I don't need another partner. I've got this."

Park ranger Vivian Hollister rose from a wooden chair and began to pace around her supervisor's small office. Beyond the open blinds, she could see the parking lot in front of the headquarters building was empty. Her fellow rangers had already headed out to patrol their allotted areas, while she'd been ordered to remain behind for a private meeting with Mort.

"Look, Viv, I'll be the first to admit that you're damned good at your job. You've been here at Lake Pleasant for a long time and I've never had to worry about you slacking off, or making a wrong decision about handling problems. But—"

Vivian didn't allow him to finish. "But what? I've been here nine years, Mort. Going on ten. And by that length of time, you should know I have the routine down. Why bother bringing someone in to fill Louis's place when I can handle the job on my own?"

The sixty-year-old man with red hair was tall and raw-boned, with blue eyes that crinkled at the corners. He'd been Vivian's supervisor from the day she'd been hired on at Lake Pleasant State Park in Arizona. Since then, he'd not only been a great boss, but he'd also become her friend, and she'd expected him to understand her reluctance to work long days with a stranger. Instead, his patient smile made it clear she was wasting time trying to argue her point.

"If Louis was only going to miss a day or two of work, I'd say fine, Viv. Go ahead and handle it on your own. But at the very least, it's going to be four to six months before Louis's broken leg will be ready for work again. And with the Christmas holiday coming up, the park is going to be brimming with extra campers. Like it or not, you're going to need help."

Vivian's jaw dropped as she turned to stare at her boss. "Six months! I talked to Louis over the phone yesterday morning. He told me he'd be back at work in two or three weeks!"

Mort shook his head. "That was before the doctor discovered the tibia bone in Louis's leg was more than a stress fracture. It's going to require surgery to fix it. If things go well and Louis takes care of himself, he'll be back to work by spring."

Vivian stifled a groan. Today was the second day of December. Spring seemed like eons away. She couldn't survive without Louis for that length of time.

Completely deflated by this turn of events, Vivian wilted into the chair she'd vacated moments earlier. "Oh, no," she muttered. "Six months. Poor Louis."

"No need to worry about Louis. While he's laid up Inez will spoil him rotten. It's filling his spot here at work that's my concern right now." Mort glanced at a large clock positioned on the wall to his right. "And I'd say your new partner should be arriving any minute now."

His unexpected announcement caused Vivian to bounce up from the chair. "This morning? Now? Are you kidding me?"

Mort was about to make some sort of reply when a knock had Vivian whirling away from the supervisor's desk to stare in horror-like fascination at the door. How could he have sprung such a surprise on her? Why hadn't he warned her that she'd be meeting a new partner today? At the very least, she would've had time to mentally prepare herself.

"Come in," Mort called out.

With her hands behind her, Vivian unconsciously wrapped her fingers around the edge of Mort's desk in an effort to brace herself. Man or woman, young or old, this couldn't be good, she thought. Louis was the only partner she'd ever had. He'd always been like a father figure to her and she trusted him implicitly. She didn't want to share long working hours with a stranger.

She sensed Mort rising from his desk chair, but after that everything in the room suddenly faded, except for the man walking through the doorway. Even if she'd had time to think, he was like nothing she could've imagined for a partner.

Somewhere in his late twenties, he was tall and lean, with bronze skin, blue-black hair and black eyes hooded beneath a pair of black brows. High cheekbones and a hawkish nose dominated his angular features, yet it was the faint curve of his thin lips that caught and held her attention.

Who was this man? Rangers from other areas of the state sometimes visited Lake Pleasant headquarters, but if this man had been one of them, she would've definitely remembered. Just looking at him made her feel hot all over.

"Sawyer, good to see you," Mort greeted as he went to shake the man's hand. "And right on time, too."

"Nice to see you again, Mr. Woolsey," he said as he gave Mort's hand a hearty pump. "I had planned to be here earlier, but a rancher on the res decided this morning was a good time for a cattle drive down the highway."

"No worries about the time. And you needn't bother with the Mr. Woolsey. Just call me Mort, like everyone else around here. Except for Viv. She calls me Mort, plus a few other things I'd rather not repeat," he joked, then motioned for Vivian to join them. "Come here, Viv, and let me introduce you to your new partner."

Certain she'd suddenly walked into some sort of hazy dream, Vivian drew in a deep breath and forced herself to move toward the two men.

"Viv, this is Sawyer Whitehorse. He'll be working with you until Louis is back on his feet. And, Sawyer, this is Vivian Hollister."

The man flashed a smile at her and extended his hand. Vivian fought off the urge to wipe her sweaty palm on the hip pocket of her twill pants and offered him her hand.

"It's a real pleasure to meet you, Ms. Hollister," he said. "From what I hear, it's going to be tough trying to fill Louis's shoes. But I'll do my best."

In spite of the cold weather outside, his hand felt as warm as a sunbaked rock and just as hard.

"Hello, Mr. Whitehorse. I—uh, didn't learn until just a moment before you walked in that I was getting a new partner. But now that you're here, welcome to Lake Pleasant State Park. I hope you'll enjoy your time here."

As he was still hanging on to her hand, his smile deepened and Vivian didn't miss the dimple carving his right cheek. Was there anything unattractive about the man? she wondered. So far she'd not seen it.

Beneath the hunter green jacket with ranger patches adorning the upper arms, she could see that his shoulders were very broad, while his chest narrowed down to a trim waist. The trousers of his matching green uniform hugged narrow hips and long muscled thighs that evoked images of strength and stamina.

Darn it. Sawyer Whitehorse was wearing the same uniform that every other park ranger at Lake Pleasant wore, so why did he make it look so downright sexy?

He said, "Thank you, Ms. Hollister. I'm looking forward to it."

Seemingly pleased with this new pairing of employees, Mort grinned. "Don't you two think you ought to lighten things up and make it Vivian and Sawyer? The park guests might find it a bit odd to hear you addressing each other as Ms. and Mr."

"That's fine with me," Sawyer said with another wide grin aimed at Vivian.

Was that a gleam in his dark eyes? Dear Lord, what was this man thinking? Didn't he realize she was several years older than him? Besides that, she was going to be his working partner for the next six months, not a sex object.

"Please call me Vivian," she said, while purposely extricating her hand from his warm grip.

"Well, that's better," Mort said with approval. "I think—" Before he could finish, the phone on his desk rang. "Excuse me. This call is important. You two don't need me to tell you what to do. Viv, show him around and get him acquainted with everything."

Mort left them to go deal with the phone call and Vivian walked over to fetch her jacket and hat from a hall tree standing near the front entrance of the office.

As she started to jam her arm into the sleeve, Sawyer quickly came up behind her to assist her with the garment. As his hands smoothed the fabric over her shoulders, an odd flutter attacked the pit of her stomach.

None of her fellow rangers had ever done such a gentlemanly thing for her. To them she was no different just because she was a female. And that was the way she wanted it. Until this moment. Until Sawyer Whitehorse had walked through the door with his long, lean body and sinfully sexy grin. Something about this man treating her like a lady made her feel ridiculously special.

Get a grip, Viv. You haven't had a man on your mind in years. You sure don't need to let yourself start thinking about this one. He's nothing but tall trouble.

"Thanks," she murmured, then turned to face him. "Are you ready to head out, or is there anything you need to deal with here at headquarters first?"

"I'm ready. Just lead the way."

When he'd first walked through the door, she'd thought his eyes were black like his hair. But now that she was up close, she could see they were the color of a rich coffee bean polished to a warm brown hue. The lashes surrounding them were thick and black and matched the brows that were presently arched with something very close to amusement.

Vivian levered her hat over her long, chestnut hair and tightened the stampede string beneath her chin. "I hope Mort told you that I rarely come back to headquarters for lunch. Mine and Louis's section of the park is too far away to waste the time and gas. I hope you brought something with you."

"It's in my vehicle. I usually try to think ahead."

He jammed his hat onto his head, then opened the door and gestured for her to precede him. As Vivian brushed past him, she caught the faint scent of soap and sage and some other spicy scent that was uniquely male. The fragrance evoked images of wild wilderness and making love next to a low-burning campfire.

Oh, my, where did that kind of erotic thought come from? And how was she possibly going to survive one day with Sawyer Whitehorse? Much less four to six months?

Shoving the questions aside, Vivian stepped through the doorway, while keenly aware of Sawyer following right behind her.

Outside, the sun was shining in a clear blue sky, but the north wind was crisp, even for December in Arizona. Vivian zipped the front of her jacket all the way to her throat as she walked briskly toward the SUV parked to the left of the building. Sitting next to it was a black Ford truck. Since she'd not seen the vehicle before, she could only assume it belonged to Sawyer.

"I'll get my lunch and be right with you," he said, his long stride easily keeping pace with her shorter one.

"Sure," she said. "I'll wait for you in the SUV."

He veered off to collect his things from the truck and Vivian hurried on to take her place behind the steering wheel of the work vehicle. By the time Sawyer joined her, she already had the motor running and her seat belt snapped in place.

After placing his lunch bucket and a pair of leather gloves behind the seat, he paused to look at her. "Do you normally drive?"

She stared at him. "What kind of question is that?"

He grinned and the sight of all those straight white teeth gleaming against his dark skin made her breathing go haywire. She wasn't sure whether she needed to pull in a lungful of oxygen or blow it out.

He said, "From the indignant look on your face, you think it's a sexist one."

"No! I mean, that isn't what I'm thinking," she told him. "I— Actually, I'm thinking now—before we get started— would be a good time for us to have a talk."

He settled back in the seat and folded his arms comfortably against his chest. Vivian tried not to notice the way his biceps strained the sleeves of his jacket, or the empty ring finger on his left hand.

You really didn't expect the man to be married, did you, Vivian? He has the look of a wild mustang stamped all over him.

"Okay, Vivian. Talk on. I have as much time as you do."

He made her name sound like sweet cream dripping over a ripe strawberry. Which made it even more impossible to gather her jangled senses.

"All right," she said, then, resisting the urge to lick her lips, she searched for the right place to start. "Like I said back in Mort's office, I didn't know you'd be coming today. Or any day, for that matter. This whole notion of me getting a new partner has thrown me. I was expecting to be going it alone."

His brown eyes were roaming her face, yet Vivian purposely avoided locking gazes with him. Instead, she focused on the faint curve of his lower lip and the tiny cleft denting the bottom of his chin. He'd clearly shaved this morning. His bronze skin was smooth without the hint of a whisker and Vivian couldn't help wondering how it would feel to rub her cheek against his.

"Is that what you wanted?" he asked. "To work alone?"

She cleared her throat and tried to gather her thoughts. "Not exactly. You see, Louis believed his leg was only slightly cracked and he'd most likely be back on the job in two or three weeks. Learning to work with someone new takes time and—"

"Patience," he finished for her.

"Well, yes, I suppose that's the right word for it. And I thought handling things on my own would be easier."

"Have you had many partners since you became a ranger?" he asked.

"Only Louis. What about you?"

"Three. The first one retired. The second one moved to the northern part of the state. And now I have you."

The way he said *you* very nearly made Vivian shiver. She reached for the knob that adjusted the heater and turned it up a notch. "I see. So how long have you been a ranger?"

"Nine years," he answered. "I became a ranger right after I turned twenty."

She'd guessed him to be in his late twenties and she'd guessed right. And though his age really had nothing to do with anything, it made her feel ridiculously old.

"There's a tiny crease marring your forehead," he said. "What's the matter? Is there anything wrong with me being twenty-nine?"

"No. It's just that you're very young." *Compared to me*, she almost added.

He studied her for a long moment before he finally asked, "How long have you been a ranger?"

"Nine years for me, too. Only I didn't start as young as you. I'm thirty-five."

He shrugged as though her age was insignificant and she supposed, to him, it was.

"You didn't have to tell me your age," he said, then flashed her a grin that was far too provocative. "But if it makes you feel any better you look a lot younger."

She stared at him in disbelief while the urge to curse

and laugh fought a duel inside her. "Is that supposed to be a compliment?"

"Just the facts, ma'am."

There was a teasing lilt to his voice and it warned her that if she didn't try to put a brake on his behavior right now, he would soon be outright flirting. And she couldn't deal with that. Not from this man.

She squared around in the seat until the seat belt was straining tightly against her shoulder. "Look, Sawyer, I have no idea if your former work partners were male or female. Or what sort of relationship you had with them. But I think you need to know right up front, right now, that there isn't going to be any flirting, any hanky-panky or anything else between us. The only thing the two of us are going to do together is…work. Got it?"

"That's what I'm here for—work," he said cheerfully. "I know the ranger rules. Hands off. No flirting. No hanky-panky. No anything else."

He was making fun of her. Making her sound like some prim spinster afraid to have a man even look in her direction. Damn it.

He said, "You know, you're even prettier when you get stirred up."

Her jaw tight, she stared out the windshield. Damn, Mort. What in the hell was he thinking calling in a man like this to take Louis's place? Why couldn't he have called some man out of retirement, some old ranger that didn't set her on fire each time she looked at him?

"What makes you think I'm stirred up?"

Leaning slightly toward her, he studied her face. "Because the little gold flecks in your green eyes are flashing fire and there's a raspberry-red color staining your cheeks."

What was it about this guy? She wanted to be outraged

and insulted, yet deep down she felt flattered that he was implying she was attractive.

Oh, brother, she'd been without a man for much too long. At least, that's what her younger brother Holt would say.

"Really?" she asked.

"Sure. We're going to be the best of partners," he said, then gestured toward the gearshift. "Don't you think you should put that in Reverse and get us out of here? We're burning daylight."

Straightening away from him, she yanked the gearshift into R and tromped on the gas pedal to send the vehicle flying backward. If Mort happened to look out the window and see gravel spewing from the tires, then so be it, she thought crossly. He was the one who'd gotten her into this mess.

Chapter Two

Sawyer would be lying if he said he was anything but shocked when he'd walked into Mort Woolsey's office and found Vivian Hollister waiting for him.

When he'd been contacted about taking the temporary position here at Lake Pleasant, he'd been excited at the opportunity to work in different surroundings. He'd not bothered to ask who he'd be working with. And even when Mort had told him his new partner would be a woman, he'd not been fazed one way or the other. Sawyer liked to think of himself as easygoing and flexible. He could work with most anyone. And he'd expected Vivian Hollister to be no different. Still, he'd imagined his new partner was going to be a coarse, homely woman in her early fifties with a henpecked husband waiting for her at home.

Vivian Hollister had blown that image to smithereens. Tall and shapely with chestnut-red hair that brushed her shoulders, she had the face of an angel and the sass of an unbroken filly. Just looking at her sent his thoughts in all sorts of naughty directions. And to make matters worse, she knew it.

As for the husband waiting on her at home, he wasn't sure about that yet. Back in Mort's office, he'd checked out her ring finger and there definitely hadn't been any sort of band or diamonds to brand her as some man's wife. But that hardly meant she was unattached. For all he knew, she could have a special boyfriend, or even a live-in lover. No doubt, a woman who looked like her had men circling around her like a pack of hungry coyotes.

"Where did you work before?"

Her question brought him out of his daydreaming and he looked over to see her focus was on the narrow blacktopped road. So far they'd been traveling through open desert hills dotted with spiny bayonet, sage, cacti and agave. To his right, in the far distance, he caught glimpses of blue water.

"At Dead Horse Ranch State Park. It's near Cottonwood. Are you familiar with the area?"

"A little. Enough to know the landscape is far different up there than it is here. You have trees and forests and creeks. We mostly have thorns, horned lizards and rattlesnakes. Are you sure you can handle it until spring ends?"

He chuckled. "I can handle most anything—for a while."

"If you live in Cottonwood, you have a long commute," she commented.

"I live on the Yavapai-Apache reservation west of Camp Verde. Once I get on 17 the drive isn't all that bad."

She darted him a glance. "You have family there? On the reservation?"

"Only my grandmother. I live with her."

"Oh."

His gaze slipped over her profile to eventually land on

the soft, sweet curve of her lips. Did she have a special man that kissed her until she was wrapping her arms around his neck and begging for more?

Trying to shake off that image, he repeated her one-word reply. "Oh. What does that mean? You can't figure why I'd live on the reservation?"

"No. It means I'm a bit surprised that you live with your grandmother. I figured you'd have a bachelor pad in town."

Chuckling again, he shook his head. "Me live in a town? Never. And I'd never leave my grandmother. She raised me from a little boy. It's time for me to take care of her now."

She shot him an odd look that he couldn't quite decipher. Maybe she considered it strange, even shiftless, for a man of his age to still be living with his grandmother in the same house he'd grown up in. Some of his friends thought so. They'd often encourage him to move off the reservation so that he'd be closer to his work and all the excitement and entertainment the city had to offer. But none of them understood what he deemed most important in his life.

"Is your grandmother elderly?"

"Nashota is seventy-seven. And thankfully in great health. When I said take care of her—I didn't mean she was decrepit. I meant financially and to make sure she knows that she's loved and has a purpose for living. That kind of thing."

She remained quiet for a long time, and though Sawyer would've liked to know what was going on in that pretty head of hers, he didn't ask. It wasn't often that he talked to a woman about his grandmother or his personal life. And he wasn't sure why he'd said anything to Vivian Hollister. But there was something soft and alluring about her that tugged at him. Something that made her very different from the women he normally associated with.

After a moment, she said, "You're a lucky man, Sawyer. All of my grandparents have passed on. I miss not being able to spend time with them."

She understood. And he suddenly realized Vivian Hollister was far more than a pretty female in a ranger uniform. The knowledge left him a little uneasy. It wasn't in his nature or his plan to ever get serious about a woman. And he definitely didn't want to develop an important attachment to this one.

Hell, why would he be worrying about such a thing? He was an expert at playing the field. He knew how to enjoy a woman without letting his heart take a serious dive. Enjoying some romantic time with Vivian shouldn't put him in a risky situation. He wouldn't let it.

"That's why I want to be around for these last years of her life. Some of my friends call me corny and a few other things. For being so close to my grandmother. But that's all right. I have a tough hide."

"I wouldn't call your devotion corny. I'd call it admirable."

Admirable. Sawyer couldn't remember ever being called that by anyone before. Especially a woman. Granted, he was basically a good guy. But he was hardly one to be admired. It wouldn't be long before Vivian figured that out for herself. Still, for now, he might as well enjoy her approval for as long as it lasted, he thought.

He forced his gaze to move away from her and on to the landscape passing the passenger window. "Is this the route you and Louis usually patrol?"

"This is it. There's nearly a hundred and fifty camping sites in the park, so the responsibilities for those are divided among the rangers. This is the area Louis and I keep tabs on. Along with several hiking trails."

"What about the lake itself? I understand there are sev-

eral water sports going on around here for most of the
year."

"That's right. Fishing, boating, scuba diving and swim-
ming. Our duties don't include visitors on the water. The
park has specially trained rangers for that job. So we don't
have to concern ourselves with those folks." She wheeled
the SUV onto a curved blacktopped road that entered
a large camping area. "I don't know about Dead Horse
Ranch State Park, but you can see we have lots of snow-
birds during the winter months."

As she drove very slowly through the campgrounds,
Sawyer eyed the motor homes and camp trailers parked
on the desert hillside. A few mesquite trees and tall saguaros dotted the landscape, along with a variety of cacti
and thorny chaparrals. The rugged landscape appealed to
Sawyer. Almost as much as the woman sitting beside him.

"Do you have many problems with visitors carving into
the saguaros or that sort of thing?"

"Most of the park visitors understand the rules not to
disturb the trees or vegetation. But from time to time there
are some who decide it's more fun to vandalize than to
enjoy the beauty of nature."

"Same at Dead Horse Ranch. I might as well tell you
that it doesn't bother me to write those kinds of people a
ticket."

She glanced at him. "It doesn't bother me, either. Honest
mistakes are a different matter. Especially when children
make them. But to me, deliberate acts are unpardonable."

She sounded as though she could be firm when needed
and flexible when the situation warranted. Thank goodness she didn't sound like one of those gung-ho rangers,
who considered themselves more as deputy sheriffs rather
than park protectors.

He glanced out the window just as they passed a site

with an elderly man cooking at a built-in grill. "Kind of cold to be cooking breakfast outside this morning," Sawyer commented. "I take it the park doesn't have a fire ban on right now."

"No. If at all possible, we try to avoid fire bans. Visitors especially enjoy cooking out. And folks from the northern states think this sort of weather is warm."

He chuckled. "Right. T-shirts in forty-degree weather. We see the same thing at Dead Horse Ranch," he said, then glanced in her direction. "Do you live close by? Or do you have a long commute to work?"

"I live a few miles out of Wickenburg. So the drive isn't all that bad."

He waited with hopes she'd add something more about her personal life. To his disappointment, she remained silent so he asked, "No other rangers from that area to carpool with?"

"No. What about you?"

He shook his head. "Not that I know of. Anyway, I'm independent. I like to come and go on my own."

She looked at him and smiled and Sawyer decided for the next six months he was going to have a hell of a time trying to keep his mind on his work. There was something totally sexy about the way the corners of her lips tilted upward and her green eyes glimmered like sunlight on the water.

"Me, too," she said, then her expression turned thoughtful. "Maybe we have more in common than I first thought."

He tried not to grin, but he couldn't help it. She made him feel very happy that he was a man. And as of this morning, a very lucky man. "Oh, I expect we're going to discover we have a lot in common, Vivian."

The tone of his voice must have given his thoughts away

because she suddenly rolled her eyes and focused her attention back to her driving.

She said, "As long as the hanky-panky isn't one of the things we have in common, then we'll get along fine."

He laughed. "Oh, Vivian. You're so prim and pretty."

Shaking her head, she said, "And you're so—ridiculous."

"Oh, come on. You know you want to laugh with me. And you know you already like me. Don't you?"

He could see the corners of her lips twitching as she fought to hold back a smile.

"Stop it. Stop it right now," she ordered in a voice that was more playful than demanding.

"No. You stop, Viv, right now."

Her head jerked in his direction and she frowned at him in stunned fascination. "What?"

"Back up. To the campsite we just passed on my side. The guy was changing the oil in his truck."

"That's not exactly a crime, Sawyer," she pointed out.

"No. But I want to make sure he doesn't think he's going to dispose of all that used oil back at the sanitary station."

"I hadn't thought about that," she admitted. "And I should have. We've caught people trying to dump all sorts of environmental hazards into the sewer tank. Hopefully this guy plans to haul the oil to the nearest town and dispose of it properly."

"We're going to make sure he does."

Vivian jammed the vehicle in Reverse and slowly backed to the entrance of the campsite.

"I'll let you deal with this one," she said smugly, as the two of them climbed out of the SUV. "You're the one who spotted it."

"Thanks," he said drily. "I always like to start my day off being a jerk."

"Don't you mean doing your duty?" she asked, as she walked alongside him.

Sawyer looked at her and chuckled. "Sometimes they're one and the same."

He'd called her Viv. Such a simple little thing that really meant nothing. And yet, here it was nearly three hours later and Vivian still couldn't quit thinking about the way his shortened use of her name had made her feel. The way *he* made her feel. It was crazy.

"Do you always eat like a bird?"

He was sitting a few feet away from her on a sunbaked boulder just off a hiking trail. Less than three yards in front of them was the edge of a rock bluff overlooking a portion of the lake. It was a beautiful view of the water among the desert hills, and they'd chosen the spot to stop for lunch.

For the past fifteen minutes Vivian had watched him wolf down two sandwiches, a bag of chips and a banana. Now he was topping it off with a chocolate cupcake with thick confectioner's icing. As for her, she'd managed to nibble her way through half of a bologna sandwich, but even eating that much food had been a major chore. Being in Sawyer's company had caused major butterflies in her stomach. At this rate, she'd be skin and bones before Louis came back to work.

"Normally I have a big appetite. I'm just not hungry for lunch today. Guess I had too much eggs and chorizo for breakfast."

"You cook breakfast before you leave for work?"

No, Vivian rarely cooked anything. Not because she disliked it, but because Reeva, the longtime house cook for Three Rivers Ranch, always kept delicious dishes on the family table. But Vivian wasn't quite ready to reveal to Sawyer that she and her daughter lived with her mother and brothers on one of the largest ranches in Arizona. He saw her only as a working woman. And for now that was the way Vivian wanted to keep it.

"I cook whenever the urge hits me." Which was true enough, she thought.

"Guess your husband enjoys it whenever you do make his favorite meal."

His remark was more than obvious and the idea that he was interested in her marital status was flattering, along with disturbing.

"I wouldn't know," she replied. "I've not seen him in more than eleven years."

Even though he'd slipped on a pair of aviator sunglasses earlier this morning, she could tell he was staring at her. The idea made her want to jump to her feet. Instead, she wrapped up what was left of her sandwich and stuffed it back into her lunch bucket.

"I take it he's an ex-husband."

"That's right," she said stiffly. "I was married for two years. Long enough to have a daughter."

He continued to stare at her and Vivian wondered what he was thinking. Most likely that he wasn't going to waste his time flirting with a single mother in her midthirties. And he'd be thinking right. She wasn't in the market for a man. Even if her family was often pushing her to find one.

Her family couldn't understand her aversion to getting back into the dating scene. After nearly twelve years of being single, most of them figured she was over her short, disastrous marriage. Her little brother Holt was the only one who seemed to understand her feelings about risking her heart again. Not because he'd been married before, but because out of all her siblings, she was closest to him and he to her. Holt recognized that it wasn't men Vivian mistrusted, but rather her own judgment of them.

"You have a daughter?"

"Yes. Hannah. She's twelve going on thirteen. Although, to hear her tell it, she knows more than a twenty-year-old."

He grunted with amusement. "Don't we all at that age?"

She cast him a wry smile. "I suppose. I remember I was around that age when I told my mother I was going to be an astronaut and nothing could stop me."

"Obviously something stopped you."

She let out a soft laugh. "I got on an airplane with my two older brothers for a trip to California. Once the plane landed I was so terrified I begged them to rent a car for the return trip. They refused and I hid my eyes during the entire flight back home."

He grinned. "So you learned you didn't like leaving the ground."

"I figured out exploring the desert is much more fun to me."

"Most women like office jobs. What made you decide to be a park ranger?"

She shook her head. "I'm not the indoor type. And my parents pushed all of us kids to get at least some college education, so I studied for four long years and ended up with a degree in natural resource management and nearly enough hours for a degree in agribusiness. Later on—after I divorced—I was glad that I'd acquired all that knowledge. It was just what I needed to get a job here at Lake Pleasant."

"Hmm. You've got me beat in the education department. I'm still working toward my degree in wildlife ecology. A few more online courses and I should be finished by the end of this coming spring."

Just about the time Louis would be returning, she thought. By then she'd either be very glad to see Sawyer go, or very sorry. At the moment it was too early to predict how she'd be feeling about telling him goodbye.

"I'm sure you'll be excited to get that behind you. Are you planning to stay at Dead Horse Ranch after you get your degree?"

He nodded. "Next year a management job will be opening up. I'll need my degree to have a shot at it."

"And you want to work at a park that doesn't take you far away from your grandmother," she stated.

He crumpled the empty cupcake wrapper and stuffed it into a sack with the rest of his lunch trash. "That's right. Lake Pleasant is really farther away from the reservation than I'd like to be. But this job is only for a few months and Nashota, that's my grandmother, insisted I take it. See, she has a mystical nature and something told her that my time here will bring me good fortune."

"You believe in that sort of thing?"

A crooked grin slanted his lips. "I believe in Grandmother. Because I sure as heck can't argue with her. She has a stubborn streak."

He made talking to him oh, so easy. And that was dangerous, she thought. If she wasn't careful, she'd soon be telling him things about herself that were better kept locked away.

She turned her gaze away from him and tried to focus on a giant agave plant growing off to her right. "I don't know what kind of good fortune you might find around here," she said, "but it doesn't hurt to dream."

He asked, "Do you ever think about asking to be transferred to a different park?"

The question brought her gaze back to him. "Not ever. I've never lived away from my family. It would take something very special for me to ever move away."

In spite of the sunglasses covering his eyes, she could

tell his gaze was thoughtfully searching her face. Which surprised Vivian somewhat. So far, Sawyer seemed to be a lighthearted jokester, who appeared to consider flirting nothing more than a fun game.

"You have family living in Wickenburg?"

Thankfully he hadn't yet connected the Hollister name to Three Rivers Ranch. And for today, at least, Vivian was glad he didn't know she was an heiress to a cattle empire.

"Yes. A mother, four brothers, two of whom are older than me, and a younger sister. My sister is currently living away, though."

"You didn't mention a father. What about him? Or is that question too personal?"

She very nearly laughed. He'd talked about her lips being kissable. Could he get any more personal than that?

"No. It's not too personal," she told him. "I didn't mention Dad because he's been dead for several years. A horse accident."

"Oh. Sorry."

She sighed. Officially, Joel's death had been ruled an accident, but as far as the family was concerned, there was too much mystery surrounding the incident to pass it off as an accident. But she'd only met Sawyer a few hours ago. She didn't know him well enough to share the few facts they had about her father's death with the man.

"Yes. I still miss him terribly." Her voice strained to speak around the lump in her throat. "What about you? Do you have siblings?"

"No brothers. No sisters. It's only me and Nashota. My dad died when I was eight years old—a construction accident. After that happened, my mother moved away with another man. I've never seen or heard from her since."

Looking at this strong and striking man, it was very difficult to imagine him growing up without a father and a mother who'd basically chosen to desert him. Given that sort of childhood, it was commendable that he'd turned into a responsible man.

"That's tough."

He shrugged. "Life is often tough. More for some than for others. I happen to think I was lucky. I had Grandmother to grab me by the seat of the pants and keep me on a straight path. Some of my childhood friends didn't have as much. I wouldn't want to tell you how they've ended up."

This morning his playful flirting had made her uncomfortable, yet surprisingly this genuine side of him disturbed her even more. The idea of him wanting, hurting and needing in the most basic human ways touched her more than he could ever guess.

"Yes. Lucky you." She rose from her seat of slab rock. "We'd probably better be going. We still have one more hiking trail to cover before we hit another set of campgrounds."

While she gathered up her partially eaten lunch, Sawyer left his seat and walked over to the edge of the bluff.

"This is an incredible view," he said. "From this distance the saguaros look like green needles stuck in a sand pile."

She looked over to see the strong north wind was hitting him in the face and molding his uniform against his muscled body. The sight of his imposing figure etched against the blue sky and desert valley caused her breath to hang in her throat.

She walked over to where he stood, then took a cautious step closer to the ledge in order to peer down at the view directly below.

"I never get tired of it," she admitted. "There are a few Native American ruins not far from here. We'll hike by those before we finish our route."

A hard gust of wind suddenly whipped across the ledge and caused Vivian to sway on her feet. Sawyer swiftly caught her by the arm and pulled her back to his side.

"Careful," he warned. "I wouldn't want you to topple over the edge."

With his hand on her arm and his sturdy body shielding her from the wind, she felt very warm and protected. And for one reckless moment, she wondered how it would feel to slip her arms around his lean waist, to rise up on the tips of her toes and press her mouth to his. Would his lips taste as good as she imagined?

Shaken by the direction of her runaway thoughts, she tried to make light of the moment. "That would be awful," she agreed. "Mort would have to find you another partner."

"Yeah, and she might not be as cute as you."

With a little laugh of disbelief, she stepped away from his side. "Cute? I haven't been called that since I was in high school. I'm beginning to think you're nineteen instead of twenty-nine."

He pulled a playful frown at her. "You prefer your men to be old and somber?"

"I prefer them to keep their minds on their jobs," she said staunchly. "And you are not *my* man."

His laugh was more like a sexy promise.

"Not yet."

Chapter Three

Later that night in the big family room on Three Rivers Ranch, the Hollisters were enjoying drinks before dinner when Hannah plopped down on the couch next to Vivian.

Eyeing the beseeching grin on her daughter's pretty face, Vivian said, "Okay, I know that look. What are you wanting? To add something to your Christmas list?"

Hannah wrinkled her pert little nose. "Oh, Mom, I've only asked for two things."

"Only two? A horse and a saddle. You already have both."

"Yes, but a girl can't have too many horses or saddles," her daughter pointed out, then gave her long blond braid a flip over one shoulder. "Anyway, I don't want anything else on my Christmas list. I wanted to ask if you'd take Nick and me down to Red Bluff this weekend."

Frowning, Vivian placed her drink on a nearby table, then turned her full attention to Hannah. "Red Bluff? Whatever for?"

Hannah rolled her eyes in droll fashion. "We've not been down there to see Aunt Camille in ages. And it's so warm and pretty there. We want to go riding down the canyon."

Red Bluff Ranch was another property of the Hollister family. At thirty-five thousand acres, it was only a fraction of the size of Three Rivers, but it was equally important. Located at the bottom of the state, near Dragoon, the climate remained much milder than Three Rivers. Each autumn her oldest brother, Blake, who managed the family ranch, shipped several hundred head of cow/calf pairs to Red Bluff for winter grazing.

"It's a long drive to Red Bluff and I don't want to haul two horses that far just for a weekend trip."

Scooting closer, Hannah grabbed her mother's hand and squeezed it tightly. "But you wouldn't have to haul the horses. Matt says Daisy and Dahlia are down there. We can ride them."

The two paint mares were sisters and perfectly suitable for her daughter and nephew to ride. Which meant she had one less excuse to avoid making the trip. "I'm not sure Camille would want our company."

"Yes, she would. She told me that she gets lonely down there by herself."

"If she gets that lonely she'd come home and live with her family," Vivian muttered, then sighed as she noticed the disapproving look on her daughter's face. "Okay, I shouldn't have said that."

Hannah shook her head. "It wasn't nice, Mom. You just don't like it because Aunt Camille wants to live down there instead of up here with all of us. That's her choice."

That much was true, Vivian thought. She missed her younger sister. She also thought Camille was making a mistake by running and hiding from her personal problems.

But she wasn't going to discuss those matters. Hannah already knew too much about everyone and everything.

"You're right and I'm sorry," Vivian said. "So about this trip that you and Nick have conjured up, what do his parents think about it?"

Before the girl could answer, Nick, who was one year younger than Hannah, suddenly appeared in front of the couch, and from the excited grin on his face, Vivian already had her answer.

"Mom and Dad say it's okay with them if we go to Red Bluff. Are we going, Aunt Viv?"

Last June, when Blake had married widow Katherine O'Dell, he'd also become an instant father to her son, Nick. Since then, the boy had taken to ranch life like a duck to water and like Hannah, his world revolved around cattle, horses and being a cowboy. The two children were practically inseparable and, remarkable as it seemed, never fussed or fought for any reason.

She studied Nick's eager face before glancing at her daughter. "Well, I didn't have anything important planned for this weekend. And if you two have your school studies caught up, I suppose we could make a trip down there."

"Oh, wow! That's great, Aunt Viv! Thanks!"

Hannah flung herself at her mother and promptly smothered the side of Vivian's face with appreciative kisses. "Thank you, Mom! You're the best!"

"Okay, okay." Vivian laughed. "The trip is on—as long as you two don't get into trouble before Saturday morning."

"Oh, Mom, we'll be so good you're going to see halos over our heads." Hannah gave Nick a conspiring wink. "Right, Nick?"

"Right!"

Vivian glanced over to the fireplace, where Blake and Katherine were sitting close together on a love seat. Apparently the two of them had been watching her exchange with the children. Blake was giving Vivian a thumbs-up sign, while Katherine was showing her approval with a wide smile.

Besides making her daughter and nephew happy, she'd be treating Blake and Katherine to a quiet weekend, something the two of them certainly deserved. As ranch manager of Three Rivers, her brother carried a tremendous load on his shoulders. Frankly, Vivian had been surprised when he'd taken on an even bigger responsibility of a wife and son. But marriage clearly agreed with him. She'd never seen Blake looking so contented and happy.

Yes, two of her brothers were happily married now, Vivian thought wistfully. More than a year ago, Joseph and Tessa were wed in a beautiful ceremony on the front lawn of their ranch, the Bar X. The two were still madly in love and had a baby son, Little Joe, to prove it. Blake and Katherine had been married for several months, yet they continued to look at each other like dreamy-eyed newlyweds.

Vivian was thrilled for her brothers, but seeing the way they adored their wives had her often wondering if a man would ever really look at her that way, as though he would cherish and protect her for all of his life.

"There's Jazelle. Dinner must be ready," Hannah announced.

As Hannah bounced up from the couch, Vivian glanced across the room to see the young housekeeper speaking to Maureen. No doubt she was telling her that Reeva had dinner ready to be served.

You cook breakfast before you leave for work?

Sawyer's question suddenly drifted through Vivian's mind and she realized he thought of her as a regular woman, one who cooked and cleaned and cared for her own home. What would he think of her once he found out she lived with her family and for all of her thirty-five years she'd had a huge support system around her? That she was helpless or even too privileged?

"Mom? What's wrong? Aren't you coming to dinner?"

Hannah's voice penetrated Vivian's deep thoughts and she glanced around to see the room had emptied, except for her daughter and nephew, who were waiting impatiently for her to join them.

"Oh. Sorry. I was thinking about something." Rising from the couch, she slung an arm around each child. "I hope Reeva has cooked up something good tonight. Are you two hungry?"

"I'm starving!" Nick exclaimed. "We're having barbecue ribs and charro beans!"

"Sounds good," Vivian replied, even though she doubted she could muster more than four or five bites.

"Reeva says if no one wants ribs they can have menudo," Hannah chimed in. "That's what I want. With lots of onions and jalapenos!"

The Mexican soup made with tripe and hominy was touted to cure the worst of hangovers. Maybe that's what she needed to shock her appetite back to normal, Vivian thought. That, or forget she'd ever laid eyes on Sawyer Whitehorse.

A few minutes later, after everyone around the long dining table began to eat, Maureen clanked her spoon loudly against her wineglass.

"Quiet, everyone!" she called out. "Blake has an important family announcement to share with us tonight."

"Hallelujah. He's finally selling that damned one-horn bull," Chandler, the veterinarian of the family, spoke up. "I'll never have to doctor him again."

Sitting next to Vivian, Holt waved his fork through the

air. "No. He's decided the ranch needs another horse barn. One with a therapy pool."

"Sorry, brothers. You're wrong on both counts," Blake said, then slipping an arm around Katherine's shoulders, he gave her a smile that was both incredibly intimate and loving. "My wife has just learned she's expecting. The baby should arrive by the Fourth of July. So one way or another, he or she should be a little firecracker."

Hannah looked at Nick and squealed with delight. "Wow, Nick! You're going to have a brother or sister! How cool is that?"

The boy's wide grin said it all. "That's pretty cool, all right. There will be another little baby in the family to go with Joe. And I won't be an only child anymore."

"Better make sure you ask for everything this Christmas, Nick," Holt advised the boy. "Next Christmas you'll be sharing with little brother."

"I won't mind," Nick told his uncle. "Having a brother or sister is all I want."

"That's all I've ever wanted, too. But I've quit asking," Hannah said as she slanted her mother a disappointed glance. "Mom is getting too old to have a baby, anyway."

Awkward silence suddenly settled over the table and with it a chunk of heavy guilt hit the pit of Vivian's stomach. She'd made a mess of things when she'd married the wrong man and bore his child. Because of her bad choice in men, Hannah had grown up without a father and no siblings.

"Hannah, don't be mean to your mother," Holt scolded. "She'll give you a brother or sister one day. When the time is right."

Vivian cut him a grateful look, which only made him grin and shrug.

Down the table, Maureen cleared her throat and lifted

her wineglass. "Let's everyone toast to Blake and Kat and my fourth grandchild. Let's pray the little firecracker will be healthy and happy."

Everyone seconded Maureen's sentiments and as Vivian picked up her long-stemmed glass, she glanced across the table at her brother and sister-in-law.

Blake was smart, she thought wistfully. He'd married a woman who loved him utterly. Whereas she'd chosen a man who'd only been capable of loving himself.

She was swallowing a sip of wine when Holt's elbow gouged into her rib cage and she turned her head to look at him in question.

"What's wrong?" he asked under his breath.

"Nothing is wrong," she whispered back. "Why?"

"You look like you're going to burst into tears. Aren't you happy for your brother?"

She stiffened her spine. "Of course, I'm thrilled. I'm just feeling a little sentimental. That's all."

"Oh. That's all, eh?"

"Yes. That's all," she said tartly. "Now hush and eat your ribs. Or I'm going to tell everyone you've been seeing Miss Holly Goodbody."

His dark brows shot upward before he leaned his mouth closer to her ear. "Her name isn't Goodbody. And for your information, I've not been seeing Holly."

"Hmmp. That's not what I've been hearing."

She turned her attention back on her plate, only to have Holt's elbow puncturing her ribs once again.

"What?"

"Nothing," he said. "Except that it's okay if you want another baby, you know."

From out of nowhere, a tiny pain of loss and sadness settled over her. "Holt, don't talk to me about babies. I'm not even married."

He grinned. "Who said you had to be?"

She rolled her eyes at her brother, then purposely turned her attention back to her plate.

"You've been very quiet tonight, Sawyer. Are you unhappy that you took the job at Lake Pleasant?"

Sawyer looked across the small living room to where his grandmother sat in a wooden rocker, patiently stringing polished cedar berries and tiny turquoise and coral beads. Eventually, the string would become a necklace or bracelet to be sold at a tourist shop in Cottonwood. Nashota cared little for money. As long as she had enough for necessities, she was content. But crafting the jewelry made her feel productive and useful, and Sawyer admired her for wanting to remain that way in spite of her advancing years.

"No. I'm not unhappy. Today was very interesting. And I have new things to think about."

"That's good. So what do you think about the people you'll be working with?"

Sawyer leaned forward and placed his empty mug on a small coffee table. After a meal of beef stew, fried bread and apple pie, he was stuffed. "I haven't met all of them yet. But they seem like a nice group. My partner is a woman. Her name is Vivian, but our supervisor calls her Viv. I think because he's known her for a long time."

"And what do you call her?"

He leveled a patient grin at her. "Grandmother, what does that have to do with anything?"

"There are times I'm curious."

Nashota had never been interested about such things before. Probably because she'd watched him change his dates like a man changed his boots or jeans and could clearly see that Sawyer never intended to have a serious relationship with a woman. So why was she questioning him now? he wondered.

"What's this? You're still thinking the Lake Pleasant job is going to bring me good fortune?"

Nashota lowered the string of beads to her lap and looked at him. "There is no thinking about it. The new job is going to bring you good fortune."

He almost groaned, but managed to hold it back. Nashota took her mystical feelings very seriously and expected him to do the same.

"I'm not going to be digging for gold or silver down there, Grandmother," he gently reminded her. "I'm basically going to be doing the same job as the one at Dead Horse Ranch. The only good fortune about that is the salary I'm paid."

She stabbed him with a silent look of disappointment.

Sawyer sighed. "What's wrong? I'm just telling you the way it is."

"No. That isn't the way it is. I've taught you that good fortune has nothing to do with money or gold or silver. I expect you to remember the lesson."

"Well, I don't really think good fortune has anything to do with Vivian, either."

"Maybe. Maybe not. Time will tell us."

What was going through that wily mind of hers? Sawyer wondered. It wasn't like her to have matchmaking thoughts about her only grandchild. Heck, for as far back as he could remember, she'd never so much as suggested to Sawyer that he should find a nice girl, settle down and raise a family. No, she seemed to understand that he wasn't family man material. Not after his parents' short, disastrous marriage.

"She has a twelve-year-old daughter."

"Who?"

"Vivian. My partner. And she's been divorced for nearly that long. She didn't say this, but I got the impression he wasn't much of a husband or father."

"Maybe she wasn't much of a wife."

"You mean like Onida?" Sawyer couldn't refer to the woman as his mother. Not when she'd chosen to walk away and forget she'd ever had a son.

"Hmmp. Onida was no wife or mother."

Although Nashota rarely voiced her opinion about anyone, she'd never beat around the bush when it came to Sawyer's mother, Onida. From what he could remember, she'd not been family material, either. She'd liked to stay on the go and party. Unfortunately, Sawyer had been old enough to remember the squabbles and yelling matches between his parents. And then his father had died and everything had changed.

"Vivian is not that kind of woman. She's a good ranger."

Nodding, Nashota put the rocker into a gentle motion. "I'm happy to hear this."

Sawyer was happy, too. For the next few months, he'd be spending his days with the beautiful woman. To be handed such an opportunity was a gift. Or was it the good fortune his grandmother talked about? Either way, Sawyer planned to make the most of it.

Kat was pregnant. Blake would soon have a baby of his own. Vivian was truly happy for her brother and sister-in-law. But she had to admit, at least to herself, that the news had hit her hard. Especially when her own daughter had dubbed her too old to have a baby. Later last night, after Vivian had retired to her bedroom, she'd changed into a pair of pajamas and stood gazing at herself in the dresser mirror. Was she getting to a point in her life where she needed to forget about having more children? Had she already passed the point of starting over with a man?

The questions had haunted her until she'd finally fallen asleep. Yet even now, with Mort at the front of the room, reminding her and her fellow rangers of the upcoming holiday events to be held in the park, she still couldn't push away the melancholy mood that had drifted over her.

If it makes you feel any better you look a lot younger.

Had Sawyer actually meant that as a compliment? Or had he only been mouthing platitudes because she was his partner and he wanted to get on her good side?

The ridiculous questions were revolving around in her mind when Sawyer's hand was suddenly touching her forearm, causing her to very nearly jump off the seat of the plastic chair.

"Vivian, the meeting is over," he said.

She glanced around to see Mort had left his position behind the wooden podium, while the other rangers were already shuffling out of the conference room.

Her cheeks burning with embarrassment, she jumped to her feet and grabbed her jacket off the back of the chair. "Oh. Sorry, Sawyer. I was thinking about something."

"Obviously not the park's Christmas events," he said drily.

As she shouldered on her jacket, he reached to pull the fabric up and over her shoulders. The gentlemanly gesture shouldn't have affected her, but just as it had yesterday it rattled her. Having him touch her, even in such an impersonal way, made her acutely aware of his tall, hard body and the utterly masculine scent surrounding him.

"I didn't miss the important issues," she said, as she zipped up the front of the hunter green jacket. "Besides, this won't be my first Christmas at the park."

"It's a relief to know you're on top of things."

She darted a glance up at him, then wanted to groan at the tempting little grin on his lips.

"You look like you're perfectly capable of walking without me leading you."

Chuckling under his breath, he nudged her toward the exit. "Ouch! You're a regular little cocklebur this morning. Did you have enough coffee at breakfast?"

Actually, she'd tossed and turned for hours last night. Then, sometime after she'd fallen into a fitful sleep, the electricity had apparently blinked on and off to cause the alarm clock to miss the five o'clock buzzer. She'd overslept and barely had time to shower and dress, much less drink a cup of coffee. But she wasn't going to admit as much to this man. He'd probably remind her that she should've made sure to have fresh batteries in the clock for a backup system.

"Not exactly. But I'll be fine."

Outside, as the two of them walked to their vehicle, a cool north wind was whipping across the parking lot, while a bank of gray clouds in the western sky suggested there might be rain in store for them. But a tease was most likely all that would come from the clouds. Rain was a rare commodity in this part of the state, and snowfall even more extraordinary. The chance of seeing snowflakes was as far-fetched as the idea of her having another baby. It wasn't going to happen.

Trying to shove that dismal thought from her head, Vivian jerked a black scarf from the pocket of her jacket and tied it around her neck.

"Have you ever seen a white Christmas, Sawyer?"

"No. Have you?"

"The only time I've ever seen snow was during a trip to the San Juan Mountains in Colorado," she said.

She opened the driver's door to the SUV and slid behind

the steering wheel. Sawyer quickly settled himself in the passenger seat and she started the engine.

As he buckled his seat belt, he said, "I saw snow once. On a trip to Flagstaff. It was melting the moment it hit the ground. So I've never seen a pile of the stuff before. Can't say that I want to."

She backed out of the parking spot, then pulled onto the asphalt road leading away from headquarters. "I couldn't live in a northern state. I don't like to be cold or housed in."

"I heard once that Onida was in North Dakota."

Surprised by his out-of-the-blue comment, she glanced at him. "That's your mother?"

He grimaced. "Onida is the woman who gave birth to me. I wouldn't categorize her as a mother, though."

Vivian could understand his reasoning. If her mother had walked away from her and never returned, she'd probably be thinking in those same terms. "Did you try to search for her?"

He shook his head. "Why would I want to find her?"

"Oh, I don't know. Maybe to show her what she's missed. To show her the fine young man you've grown to be. Even without her help."

From the corner of her eye Vivian could see him shrug one shoulder, as though the woman's opinion didn't matter to him. The idea was a sad one. Nearly as sad as the thought that she'd never have the big family she'd always dreamed about.

"She's dead, Vivian."

Her gaze left the road long enough to look in his direction, but all she could see was the back of his head as he stared out the passenger window.

"You mean, literally?"

He looked at her, his expression as bland as if they'd been discussing the weather. Either he held no emotion for the woman, or he was an expert at hiding his true feelings, Vivian decided.

"Years ago, Grandmother was told by a mutual friend that she died in a car accident. But we never bothered to search for her whereabouts. Either way, she's dead to me."

Deciding it would be best to let the subject drop, Vivian remained silent as she steered the vehicle into the first campground on their work schedule.

The first three sites were quiet, prompting Sawyer to say, "Everyone must be sleeping late this morning."

"Not everyone," Vivian replied as she spotted a young woman with a blond ponytail wearing a pair of short shorts hurrying to the side of the road. Behind her, a small girl was struggling to control a leashed black-and-white dog.

When the woman began waving her arms at them, Sawyer said, "Looks like she wants us to stop."

Vivian parked in a safe spot out of the way of traffic, but before either of them could depart the vehicle, the woman raced up to Sawyer's window.

He lowered the glass and she gave him a wide smile.

"Are you two rangers?" she asked.

"That's right," Sawyer said. "I'm Ranger Whitehorse and she's Ranger Hollister. Can we help you with something?"

Even from her vantage point, Vivian could see the young woman was ogling Sawyer as though she'd just stumbled onto the most beautiful thing she'd ever laid eyes on.

"Uh—yes. Maybe you can. We wanted to go on the doggie hike or puppy walk or whatever it's called. Is it somewhere around here?"

Sawyer looked to Vivian for help. "Sorry," he said. "I haven't had a chance to go through all the park projects yet."

Leaning up in the seat, Vivian said to the woman, "Yes, it's about a quarter mile north of here. Just follow the road until you see the signs to the hiking trailhead. But you'd better hurry." She glanced at her wristwatch. "The ranger leading the group will be leaving in fifteen minutes and he's always prompt."

"Oh. Okay." She shot Sawyer another engaging smile. "I don't suppose you could give us a lift, could you?"

"No. Afraid not," he said.

"Aww, guess we'll have to hurry, then. I just hope the other ranger looks like you."

Resisting the urge to roll her eyes, Vivian started the SUV and taking the hint, the young woman stepped out of the way.

Once she'd eased into gear and started down the road, Sawyer cleared his throat and turned an amused glance on Vivian.

"Park guests will ask a ranger anything," he reasoned.

She let out a heavy breath. "I know. Over the years I've heard all sorts of things. Some of which I would never repeat."

"She was a bit ditzy, but pretty," he commented.

"You ought to be ashamed. She's probably not a day past twenty."

"What's wrong with being young?"

"Nothing." Except that Vivian had never felt more like an old biddy and she hated the feeling. And she especially hated this self-pity party she'd been having for herself ever since she'd learned Blake and Kat were having a baby.

"Is something wrong with you, Vivian?"

Unwittingly, her foot eased off the gas pedal. "Wrong? What do you mean?"

She glanced over at him and tried to ignore the way her pulse leaped at the sight of his dark profile.

"I've only known you for one day. But you're different from yesterday. A little sad, I think. Am I making you sad, Vivian?"

His words weren't necessarily intimate or provocative, and yet the way he said them made it feel as though he'd whispered them in her ear. The sensation caused goose bumps to erupt on her arms and she was thankful the long sleeves of her shirt hid them from his sight.

Swallowing, she said, "No. You aren't making me sad. Or mad. I'm just a little thoughtful this morning. That's all."

"Your eyes are dull. Yesterday they were snapping with life. They were much prettier that way."

Dear God, how did this man see so much about her? Garth had been her husband for two years, but he'd never noticed such little nuances about her eyes or mood or anything else. To know that Sawyer was observing her so closely was unsettling, to say the least.

"Sorry if I seem glum today, Sawyer. It has nothing to do with you."

Not exactly, she silently corrected. But she could hardly tell him that his young, handsome face and lean sexy body had jolted awake her slumbering senses. No more than she could admit that spending time in his company had reminded her of the many things she'd been missing these past years since her divorce.

"Good," he said. "I didn't come here to Lake Pleasant to cause you problems."

No doubt he'd caused many a woman problems. Most all of them heart related. The very kind of problems she didn't need.

"I'm going to make sure that you don't," she said primly.

He laughed and the sound relieved the tension that had been building ever since they'd left headquarters.

"I told my grandmother that you're a good woman. So far you're definitely not making a liar out of me."

The urge to pull the SUV over to the side of the road and stare at him was so strong, she had to force her hands to remain steady on the steering wheel.

"I suppose you meant that as a compliment," she stated in a voice that was meant to be casual, but even she could hear a quaver in her words.

"Nothing else."

She let out a small breath as she steered the vehicle onto a graveled drive that circled an open pavilion. "I can't believe you mentioned me to her."

"Why not? You're my new partner."

"Yes, but…"

"But what? You don't like me saying something nice about you?"

"You don't know that I'm a good woman. You only met me yesterday. That's not enough time for you to know what kind of person I really am."

"Mort likes you. That's good enough for me. Besides, my grandmother has a gift for seeing right into people. I think I inherited some of her gift."

She arched a brow at him, but said nothing until she parked at the end of the pavilion and looked over at him. "Okay. I shouldn't ask this, but what are you seeing right now—looking at me?"

"I see a woman who's sad about something in her life. She's also annoyed with herself."

Dear Lord, the man was right on both counts. Which made her wonder what else he could see about her. Not wanting to delve into his first observation, she asked, "Tell me, Mr. Mystic, why am I annoyed with myself?"

A lopsided grin lifted a corner of his lips and in spite

of Vivian's brain commanding her to look away, her gaze went straight to his tempting mouth.

"Because you don't want to like me, but in spite of your-self, you do. You've also been telling yourself you don't want to kiss me, but we both know that isn't true."

Yesterday, his bold remarks would've shocked her. But today she was only mildly surprised that he'd voiced such opinions about her. He was a flirt. A very confident one at that. And she needed to always remember that no matter what outrageous words came out of his mouth, he wasn't serious.

Forcing a playful smile on her face, she said, "I can't believe you've pegged me so perfectly. You really must have your grandmother's gift."

He laughed and after a brief moment, the happy sound had her laughing along with him. But when the laughter finally trailed away, she had to fight the urge to drop her face in her hands and weep.

"It's nice to hear you laugh, Viv."

With any luck, he wouldn't notice the soft sigh that escaped her lips. "I'm sorry for being a crab, Sawyer. Truth is, I slept very little last night."

"I hope you weren't lying awake worried about work-ing with me," he said. "We're going to be great together."

She smiled at him. "Is that prediction coming from your soothsaying abilities?"

"No. I'm not a soothsayer or anything close to it. My prediction is coming from firsthand experience."

With women, no doubt, Vivian thought wryly. Then, before she could stop herself, she blurted, "To be honest, Sawyer, you were right. I am a little sad. And I really have no reason to be. Except that last night at the dinner table, my oldest brother and his wife announced that they're having a baby."

There. She'd said it. She'd gotten it out, but rather than feeling relieved, she realized she sounded like a petulant child. Or worse. What the heck was wrong with her, anyway?

"And that made you sad? Why?" he asked curiously. "Is he unworthy of being a father?"

She shook her head. "Blake is already an excellent father. He's a strong, tender and loving man. I can't think of anyone who deserves to have children more than him."

His gaze made a thoughtful survey of her face, and Vivian felt as though his brown eyes were kissing her cheeks and lips. The erotic sensation was like nothing she'd ever felt before and she wondered if she was suffering some sort of hormonal imbalance. This wasn't normal! Nothing about the way she was reacting to Sawyer was remotely close to normal.

"Then the sister-in-law is not of your liking," he replied. "Is that what worries you?"

"No. Kat is like a sister to me. She's a wonderful mother and human being. I love her and I'm very happy for the both of them."

He shook his head as though she'd lost him somewhere along the trail.

"So you're happy and sad at the same time. That's what you're trying to say?"

"Crazy, isn't it?" she said with a self-deprecating laugh. "I should be all smiles. Instead, I want to burst into tears. Believe me, Sawyer, I don't normally behave like an emotional female. And starting right now, I'm going to put this all behind me. So let's get out and look the pavilion over. This is where Mort has scheduled the Christmas bingo party and we need to decide how many tables and chairs we can set up without crowding everyone."

"We'll get to work in a minute," he agreed. "Right now, I want to ask you something."

Determined to show him she wasn't a weak-willed sniveling female, she straightened her shoulders. "Okay. What is it? That you want to swap places with another ranger so that you can get the heck away from me?"

Clearly amused by her question, he chuckled. "No. I'm just wondering if this sadness you're feeling is really envy?"

There he went again, she thought desperately. He was putting his finger right on the sore spot in her heart.

Glancing away from him, she focused on a far distant rise, where a young couple had spent the night in a tent. At the moment they were standing at a portable grill, laughing at their feeble attempts to start a fire. Garth had never done anything outdoors with her, Vivian thought dully. But unfortunately, she'd not discovered he'd been a man averse to getting his hands dirty, until after she'd married him.

"I suppose that is what I'm feeling. You see, I always wanted a big family of my own—just like my parents had. It didn't turn out that way for me. And sometimes, well—it's hard to accept that life can be so different from what we plan."

Chapter Four

She wanted babies. Her heart was pining for a big family. The facts should've turned his red-hot attraction for Vivian into an iceberg, but nothing was freezing, especially his heart. Right now it felt like a piece of warm putty, just waiting for her to mold into whatever shape she wanted it to be.

Oh, man, if he didn't get a grip, he was going to be a goner, Sawyer thought. Everyone on the res, everyone at Dead Horse Ranch, anyone who'd ever met him for more than five minutes, knew that he wasn't stacked up to be a family man.

Hell, how could he be? For the first eight years of Sawyer's life, his father, Baul, had been too busy working to put food on the table and trying to pacify a demanding wife to pay too much attention to his son. And after he'd died, there had been no man around to teach Sawyer about being a father or husband. Besides, from what he remembered about his parents' marriage, he wanted no part of it.

Forcing his gaze away from Vivian's lovely face, he gazed out the windshield to the young couple with the tent. If the man would keep his hands to himself, the woman might be able to cook breakfast. Bet he wasn't her husband, Sawyer thought. The pair was having way too much fun to be married.

He said, "I wouldn't be feeling sad about that, Viv. You have plenty of time to find the right man and have more children."

The right man? Who was he kidding? Just saying the words had felt like he was coughing up mesquite thorns. He didn't want to think of this beauty making love to any man, except him.

She continued to look at him for long moments and then a wide smile spread across her face. "You're so right, Sawyer. I have a wonderful daughter and my life is going just fine. It's not like I need a man in my life. They're really just a nuisance, anyway."

"Thanks," he said drily.

She laughed and, though he didn't exactly know what had caused her mood to lift, he was thankful for the change.

"Oh, I didn't mean you, Sawyer. You're my coworker. I'm talking about boyfriends, husbands, lovers. I don't need that kind of drama in my life again."

You're my coworker. Clearly she wasn't thinking of him as a potential lover, Sawyer thought. But sooner, rather than later, he was going to change her mind.

"Never say never, Viv." He gave her a playful wink, then opened the passenger door. "We'd better get to work."

"Right," she agreed. "We need to be at the Indian Mesa trailhead at ten o'clock. And from the amount of campers we now have in this area of the park, I expect we'll have a big group for the tour today."

Yesterday, before the workday had ended, Sawyer and

Vivian learned that Mort had scheduled the two of them to lead a group tour this morning to the Puebloan ruins located on the north rim of the lake. The trek was something Vivian and her old partner, Louis, had done many times in the past. She knew the history of the park backward and forward, whereas Sawyer hadn't yet had time to learn his way around the park, much less study its history.

As the two of them walked toward the pavilion, he said, "Last night I took home as much literature I could find about the Hohokam ruins and crammed for a few hours."

She shot him a look of surprise. "That wasn't necessary, Sawyer."

Oh, yes, it was necessary, he thought. The last thing he wanted to do was make a fool of himself in front of this woman.

"I wanted to be prepared."

She looked over at him and smiled and Sawyer felt an odd little tug in the middle of his chest. The tender pang was like nothing he'd experienced before, making him wonder if he was suddenly turning into a sap, or something worse.

"Listen, Sawyer, don't be worried about the tour. I'm not expecting you to expertly answer questions about the ruins. You only started this job yesterday. It took me months and months to learn the history of the park. Just help me keep the visitors corralled and safe. That's all I ask."

She was trying to be nice by making it easy on him. Sawyer appreciated the fact that she wasn't being demanding. Yet he didn't warm to the notion that she considered him just a temporary ranger to fill a space until the real ranger returned. Maybe it was stupid for Sawyer's male ego to be rearing its head, but he wanted Vivian to see that he was a quick learner and that he wasn't going to spend the next six months trotting behind her while she carried the load.

"Thanks, Viv. But I'd like to contribute as much as I can."

"That's good. I just don't want you to worry. You said we're going to make a great team. And that's what we're going to be."

Her response put a grin on his face and he glanced down to see if he was actually walking on air, or if Vivian Hollister was only making him feel that way.

"Now you're talking my language," he said.

That evening after work, Sawyer was about to climb into his truck to go home when a voice from behind caused him to pause.

Looking over his shoulder at the graveled parking lot, he spotted Zane Crawford hurrying toward him. The tall, sandy-haired ranger had worked for a time at Dead Horse Ranch and during that time the two men had become friends. About a year ago, Zane had moved here to Lake Pleasant, but it wasn't until this morning in the conference room that Sawyer had spotted his old friend.

"Hey, Sawyer, I caught a glimpse of you this morning but I didn't have a chance to say hello. What the hell are you doing here, anyway? You haven't moved here permanently, have you?"

"No. Just filling in for Louis Garcia until he can return."

Zane whistled under his breath. "That might be a while. From what I hear, he nearly lost his leg."

"I don't think it was all that bad."

"That's good," Zane replied, then quickly asked, "Say, you want to go grab a bite to eat at Burro Crossing on our way home? Or do you have a date tonight?"

Sawyer chuckled. "Date? I haven't gone on a date in weeks."

Laughing now, Zane slapped him on the shoulder. "Don't try to kid a kidder, Sawyer. The last I knew you had that cute little blonde who worked in the bakery at Black Canyon City. Don't tell me you've already parted ways with her."

"Had to," Sawyer told him. "She was getting babies and picket fences on her mind."

Zane rolled his eyes. "Still the same old Sawyer."

"Come on," Sawyer said with a guilty grin. "I'll follow you to Burro Crossing."

Twenty minutes later, the two men were sitting at a window booth, sipping iced tea and waiting for their orders. Outside the bar and grill, darkness had settled over the desert hills. A trail of traffic flowing north out of Phoenix dotted I-17 with endless headlights.

"So you're working the east area of the park," Sawyer said. "How do you like it?"

Zane shrugged one broad shoulder. "Better than freezing my rear off up at the Canyon."

For a while Zane had worked the Grand Canyon Park and Sawyer hadn't envied him. Big crowds, along with freezing temperatures in the winter months, wouldn't be his thing.

"So are you and Melinda about to set the date?" Sawyer asked his friend.

The other man snorted cynically. "She returned my ring about six weeks ago. Said she needed to find herself and mentally grow before she stepped into marriage. Hell, she found another guy with a heck of a lot more money than me. That's the kind of growing she had on her mind. Guess I can just count myself lucky that she returned the ring. At least I got a hunk of change when I sold it at the pawnshop."

"Oh. Sorry, buddy. Why didn't you let me know?"

He grimaced. "It's not something I'm exactly proud of. But I'm getting over it."

"At least you didn't lose a wife," Sawyer said in an effort to comfort him.

Zane grunted. "I lost my mind for ever believing Melinda could be trusted."

"You'll get it back," Sawyer said. "Your mind, that is."

Zane looked at him, then chuckled. "Yeah. Eventually. And speaking of women, I noticed this morning that you were sitting next to Vivian Hollister. You're not trying to date her, are you?"

He planned to do more than date her, Sawyer thought. He was going to get her into his bed and keep her there just as long as he could.

"No," he answered, which was partly the truth, since dating wasn't on his mind at this very moment. "I was sitting with her because she happens to be my partner."

As Zane put two and two together, his jaw began to drop. "Oh, I must be getting slow. It's dawned on me now. I mean, about you taking Louis's place. He was Vivian's partner. Now you're working with her. Man, what's that like?"

Not knowing exactly what his friend was trying to imply with that question, Sawyer slanted him a skeptical glance. "So far, so good."

Zane's brows arched with disbelief. "That's all you have to say?"

Sawyer shrugged. "I only met her yesterday. I've not had time to get to know her."

Who are you kidding, Sawyer. You already feel like you know all the most important things about Vivian. She has a warm smile and a soft heart. She has skin that begs to be touched and lips that have you dreaming about long, hot kisses.

"Hah! You've certainly slowed down since we worked together at Dead Horse Ranch. In those days you would've already asked her out on a date. Course, she would've already turned you down, too," he added smugly.

His interest piqued by that last comment, Sawyer said, "You sound awfully sure about that. You have specific information about her that I don't? Like a special man lingering in the background?"

Zane shook his head. "I don't have any information about her personal life. As best I can tell from the few months I've worked at Lake Pleasant, she pretty much keeps her private life private. Guess that's because she's not like us regular folks. Frankly, I don't understand why she's working as a ranger. With a family like hers she could do most anything she wanted to do. Or not do."

Sawyer was trying to digest Zane's comments when the waitress arrived at the booth with their burgers and fries. He waited until she'd served them and moved away, before he picked up the conversation where they'd left off.

"Not regular folks," he repeated blankly. "I'm not understanding anything you're saying, Zane. Is Viv's family dysfunctional? Or criminal or something?"

His expression comical, Zane stared at him for several seconds and then he began to laugh and didn't stop laughing until Sawyer stabbed him with a disgusted look.

"Would you mind sharing the joke?" he asked crossly.

Quickly sobering, Zane shook his head. "Sorry, Sawyer. I couldn't help it. The fact that you honestly don't know—it blows my mind." He looked around to see if anyone was within hearing distance before he finally leaned forward and said, "It's hard to believe you haven't connected her name yet. Hollister. Think, Sawyer. The family owns and operates Three Rivers Ranch, one of the biggest ranches in Arizona."

Three Rivers Ranch. Yes, Sawyer had heard of the place. He doubted anyone living in the state wouldn't recognize the name. Still, when he'd been introduced to her, he'd not made the giant leap from her name to *those* Hollisters.

After all, working as a park ranger was the last thing he'd expect a woman of that stature to be doing.

The bite of food he'd just swallowed hit his stomach like a chunk of granite and he reached for his glass of tea.

"So you're telling me she's one of the rich Hollisters? I can't believe it. She's never so much as mentioned anything about the ranch or being a part of a family dynasty."

Zane grimaced. "Well, no. I don't figure she would. With her looks, she probably has enough problems without making things worse."

"You're talking about money now," Sawyer stated dully, while wondering why Zane's revelation had left him feeling ill. Hell, it didn't matter if Vivian was rich or poor. That didn't change the way she looked, the way she smiled at him, the way she made him feel every time he looked at her.

"What else?" Zane quipped as he dipped a fry into a puddle of ketchup. "No doubt she's always had to worry about men coming after her just as a means to get to her family's wealth."

Had that been the problem between her and her ex-husband? Sawyer wondered. Had she discovered he'd married her just for the Hollister money? On the other hand, she was a desirable woman. How could any man want money more than her? And how would she ever know what a man was really feeling about her?

The troubling questions swirling around in Sawyer's head must have shown on his face because Zane suddenly asked, "What's wrong? You honestly weren't thinking about making a play for her, were you?"

"No. Not really," he lied, while thinking his intentions, whatever they might be, weren't any of Zane's business.

"Well, I'll be the first to admit that you're good at getting women," Zane said, "but Vivian Hollister is on a whole different level than the two of us."

Technically, that was true, Sawyer decided. But whenever he was with her, it didn't feel that way. Still, working together wasn't the same as dating. She might be a real snob when it came to picking her dates.

"Doesn't matter," Sawyer said with a frown. "We're not supposed to fraternize with our coworkers."

Zane chuckled knowingly. "Since when has that rule ever stopped you?"

Hours later, in the Three Rivers ranch house, most everyone had retired for the evening when Vivian left the kitchen with intentions of going upstairs to her bedroom. She was halfway down the hallway when she spotted a shaft of light shining beneath the door of her mother's office.

Pausing, she tapped her knuckles on the closed door and stepped inside to see Maureen Hollister sitting behind a big oak desk. The same desk Vivian's father had used until his untimely death six years ago. Since that time, their mother had worked tirelessly to make sure the hundred-and-seventy-year-old ranch was thriving and her tight-knit family was healthy and happy and together. For the most part, Maureen appeared content with her life, but there were times Vivian could tell her mother was lonely.

"Mom, when are you going to quit putting in such long hours? It's nearly eleven thirty. You should be in bed," Vivian gently scolded as she moved deeper into the quiet study.

Maureen glanced up from a stack of receipts. "Look who's talking. You should be in bed, too. Five o'clock comes early in the morning."

Vivian eased into one of the green wing chairs situated in front of the desk. "I've been helping Hannah with her math. And that prompted a trip to the kitchen for a piece of the carrot cake Reeva made for dessert."

With a dry little laugh, Maureen rolled her shoulders to ease the stiffness in her neck. "You always did think doing your homework deserved a reward. If you think middle school math is a challenge, you should try going over these ranch accounts. Why is it that Jazelle only remembers half of the time to keep the grocery receipts? She's worked for us for how long now? Four years? And still, when Reeva sends her to town for supplies, she can't remember to hang on to a receipt."

"Give her a break, Mom. Jazelle is a single mother, trying to make a decent life for her little boy. She has a lot on her mind."

Sighing, Maureen reached up and pulled her thick dark hair from the ponytail she'd pulled it into early this morning. "You're right. Jazelle is a hard worker. Probably the best housekeeper we've ever had, on top of that. I won't scold her over the receipt. I'll just tell Reeva to gently remind her about them."

"You look tired," Vivian said as she observed her mother gently messaging her temples. "Did you work out on the range with the men today?"

"They were a little shorthanded and Matthew was rotating a couple of herds to different grazing areas. I spent most of the day in the saddle."

Vivian could only hope whenever she reached her early sixties, she was as strong and vibrant as her mother was now. "I'd say hire more hands, but that wouldn't keep you in the house or off a horse."

Maureen ran her fingers through her hair, then rested her head against the back of the leather executive chair. "Not in the least. But I will admit it's time to quit for the night. After I have a talk with you," she added.

"A talk about what? You see me every day and we both need to be in bed."

"I know, but we've not had a chance to talk much in the past couple of days. I wanted to ask you how Louis is doing. It's such a shame about his leg."

"I learned this morning from Mort that Louis's surgery went well. Barring any problems he'll be going home in the next couple of days. But of course he's going to need lots of rehab once everything heals."

"He's a strong man. He'll get through it. Bet you're missing him, though. You've worked with Louis ever since you became a ranger." She sighed, her expression turning wistful. "Oh, Lord, those days seem like ages ago. Your dad was so proud of you. Remember how he snapped all those pictures of you that first day you got your uniform?"

The question was moot and just her mother's way of reminiscing. Both of them were well aware that Vivian's room was full of photos her father had taken of her over the years. Not just in her ranger uniform, but riding horses, working in the cattle pens and at the chuck wagon. Joel had been exceptionally proud of his sons, while at the same time, he'd been very loving and protective of both his daughters.

"I disappointed Dad when I married Garth," Vivian said, glumly.

"You made up for it when you gave him a beautiful granddaughter," Maureen pointed out.

Joel had been crazy about Hannah, but Three Rivers had been his very life. Passed down through generations of Hollisters, he'd wanted all his children to invest their lives in the ranch. "Dad wanted me to work on the ranch. He always made his feelings clear about that. But before he died I think he'd come to realize that I was meant to be a park ranger. The job suits me."

"Of course it suits you. And the main thing Joel wanted was for his children to be happy. No matter what profession they chose."

Vivian gave her mother a wan smile. "Speaking of my job, I have a new partner now. His name is Sawyer White-horse."

Her announcement suddenly wiped the fatigue from Maureen's face. "When did this happen?" she asked eagerly. "You've not said anything."

"Yesterday morning. He walked into headquarters right before work started. Damn Mort. He sprung the guy on me without any warning. But—well, so far it's working out."

Which was putting it mildly, Vivian thought. For the past twenty-four hours her thoughts had been consumed with Sawyer. The way he looked and smelled, the sound of his voice, the power and grace in the way he moved. And that smile. Each time it spread across his face, something in the pit of her stomach quivered like partially melted gelatin.

Her interest clearly piqued, Maureen said, "Well, this is news. Is he a family man? Do you like him?"

The questions made her want to groan and laugh at the same time. How could anyone not like Sawyer? Charm oozed from the man's pores. As for being a family man, she figured he'd run from matrimony as fast and far as those long legs of his would carry him.

"Sawyer doesn't have a family. He's only twenty-nine. But I guess you could say he's sort of a family man. You see, he lives with his grandmother—it's just the two of them. And from what I can tell he's very protective of her. They live on the reservation, near Camp Verde."

"Oh. Then he must be from the Yavapai or Apache tribe," Maureen said thoughtfully.

"Apache. And Mom, the man is drop-dead gorgeous."

Her mother let out a short, quizzical laugh. "Vivian, you've surprised me. I've never heard you say that about any man. Not even Garth."

A rush of heat stung Vivian's cheeks. She'd not exactly meant to describe Sawyer in such terms, but the words had rolled out of her without resistance or forethought.

"I'm just being honest," she said with a shrug of one

shoulder. "And along with being good-looking he's a heck of a ranger."

Maureen's brows arched with skepticism. "The man has been there two days and you're already labeling him as a heck of a ranger. It's not like you to make snap judgments."

"This isn't snap, Mom. It's obvious." Scooting to the edge of her seat, she spoke with an eagerness that surprised herself as much as it did her mother. "Sawyer and I led a group to Indian Mesa today and he was wonderful. He correctly answered all kinds of questions the park visitors asked about the ruins. Not only that, along the way he pointed out a few rare plants and a small den of sidewinders. I'm telling you, Mom, I was impressed."

Maureen's expression turned indulgent. "That is supposed to be part of a ranger's job, isn't it? To answer questions about things on the park?"

"Yes, but like you said, Sawyer's only been at Lake Pleasant for two days. He doesn't know its history. He's been crash studying, though. That's how committed he is to the job."

"I can see that impresses you."

"Well, of course it does. He's only going to be at Lake Pleasant for about six months. He could just go through the motions, until he's transferred back to Dead Horse Ranch, but he's not that kind of man. He's kind of like Dad was. You know, if you don't want to give your job everything, then find a different one."

A tender smile tilted her mother's lips and in that moment, Vivian felt sad and envious at the same time. Maureen had been truly blessed to have experienced a great love with her husband, Joel. She'd given him six children, and for more than twenty-five years they'd raised their babies and worked the ranch together. To have such a great marriage cut short by Joel's death had been tragic, but on the other hand, her mother had been truly loved by a man. That was something Vivian could only dream about.

"Oh, how well I remember Joel saying those words," Maureen murmured, then leveled a soft gaze at her daughter. "I take it that you like this new ranger?"

Something fluttered in the middle of her chest. "I do. But don't worry, Mom. I don't mean like in a romantic way. Sawyer is a professed bachelor. He's also a huge flirt. He's not the kind of guy a girl gets involved with."

"You mean he's the heartbreaker kind?"

Laughing lightly, Vivian rose to her feet. "You're right on, Mom. Add to that, he's six years younger than me. And I'm hardly the cougar type."

Maureen rolled her eyes in helpless fashion. "No. You're the lonely, independent, I-don't-need-a-man-after-Garth type."

Vivian grimaced. "Okay, maybe I am all those things. But at least I can say my heart isn't breaking."

Her mother leveled a pointed look at her. "Isn't it?"

Vivian leaned a hip against the front of her mother's desk. "What does that question mean?"

"Just that since your divorce I think your heart has never stopped hurting."

Vivian groaned. "Oh, Mom, Garth turned out to be a total jerk. My heart is certainly not hurting for him."

"No. Not for him. But you've been hurting for all you've missed. Of having someone to love you and be at your side. Someone to share your life with."

Something in the middle of Vivian's chest squeezed tight enough to bring tears to the back of her eyes. "I could say the same thing about you, Mom. I'm not blind. I can see that you're lonely."

Her brows arched with fascination, Maureen leaned forward. "Me, lonely? How did you ever come up with a notion like that? I'm surrounded by family and friends and ranch hands. I have a new grandbaby and another one on the way. What more could I want?"

"You don't have Dad. You don't have a man to share your life with."

A shutter closed over Maureen's face as she hastily began to thrust stacks of receipts and statements into a bottom drawer on the desk. "I've already had the one true love of my life. At sixty-two I'm past the age of needing another man."

"Really? A person is never too old to love."

Maureen shot her a challenging look. "Then what's stopping you? Look at your two brothers. Blake and Joseph are so happy you can't wipe the smiles off their faces."

"Yes, but they're a whole lot braver than their sister Vivian. And speaking of sisters, I've promised Hannah and Nick to take them down to Red Bluff for the weekend. So we'll be seeing Camille. Anything you want to send her?"

"No. Just my love."

Vivian folded her arms across her chest as she thoughtfully studied her mother. "Why don't you want to scold her for running and hiding? Why don't you tell *her* she needs to find another man? Like you're trying to tell me?"

Locking the drawer of paperwork, Maureen rose and switched off the banker's lamp sitting on the left corner of the desk. "Because Camille hasn't wasted eleven or twelve years of her life like her sister. At least, not yet. And I don't plan to let it drag on with her."

Ignoring her mother's pointed jabs, she asked, "What do you plan to do? Force Camille to come back to Three Rivers?"

Frowning, Maureen joined her at the front of the desk. "Since when have I forced a child of mine to do anything against their will?"

"Uh, you made me wear that lavender monstrosity of

a dress to church on Easter Sunday," Vivian jokingly reminded her. "I was mortified."

"You were ten years old. And you looked adorable. As for Camille, if she likes living down on Red Bluff that's fine with me. I only want her to be happy. But if I have to do something to put a smile back on her face, I will. I just haven't figured out what that might be, but I will—in time."

Smiling coyly, Vivian leaned over and kissed her cheek. "Spoken like a true, calculating mother."

Chuckling now, Maureen dropped a kiss on the top of Vivian's head. "Good night, darling. And I'm glad to hear you like your new partner. Maybe the two of you can learn something from each other."

Vivian arched a skeptical brow at her. Sawyer could probably teach her a few things in the bedroom, but her mother didn't have that sort of "learning" in mind. Or did she?

"Learn something. Like what?"

With an arm at the back of Vivian's waist, Maureen urged her out of the room. "He's from a different park and you're from a different park. You can mesh your knowledge and experience as rangers together and make a great team."

A great team. Sawyer had already predicted the two of them would be great together. Now Vivian could only wonder what that might mean for her in the days ahead.

Chapter Five

The coffee Sawyer poured from the stainless steel thermos was hot and so was the afternoon sun beaming down on the rocky shelf where he and Vivian had stopped for a break. But the heat of the coffee, or the warmth of the sun, couldn't compare to the heat coursing through him as he furtively studied Vivian's profile.

For the past two days, ever since Zane had informed him that she was one of the Hollisters from Three Rivers Ranch, he'd been telling himself to forget his plans to get close to her. He'd be an idiot to even try to generate a relationship between them. Not unless he wanted to put himself through a humiliating rejection. And yet, even the idea of her squashing his manly pride couldn't turn off the attraction he felt for the woman.

"Tomorrow is Saturday and we both have the weekend off," he said, keeping his voice as casual as possible. "You have big plans?"

She glanced at him and Sawyer thought he spotted a

wary light in her eyes, as though she feared he was going to ask her out and she'd be put in the awkward situation of turning him down. But that wasn't his intention. Not yet.

"Actually, I do," she answered. "A few days ago I promised my daughter and eleven-year-old nephew that I'd drive them down to Dragoon for the weekend."

Sawyer rarely traveled to the southern part of the state, but he remembered Dragoon being a tiny place not far from Tombstone. What could possibly be there to interest her?

After a careful sip of coffee, he asked, "What's at Dragoon? Or is that none of my business?"

She swallowed the last bite of her cookie before she answered. "It's hardly a secret. My family owns property in the area. A thirty-five-thousand-acre ranch called Red Bluff. Presently, my younger sister is living down there. I'll have a chance to spend some time with her while Hannah and Nick ride horses around the ranch."

So the Hollisters not only owned Three Rivers Ranch, they owned a second one near Dragoon. The wealthy just got wealthier, but the news still didn't diminish the urge he felt to touch her, kiss her. Even at this moment, he wanted to scoot across the rocky ground and sit close to her side. Instead, he stared out at the blue lake water lapping at the shoreline some twenty yards away.

"A couple of days ago I learned that you live on Three Rivers Ranch."

From the corner of his eye, he watched her head turn in his direction.

"Who told you that?" she asked.

"Zane Crawford. He works the east side of the park. We've been friends for a few years."

"Oh. I'm slightly acquainted with Zane. But I'm surprised that you are. Other than Mort, I didn't think you knew any of the other rangers here at Lake Pleasant." She turned her gaze away from him before she continued. "Most everyone knows I live with my family on Three Rivers. I figured Mort had already mentioned it to you. Or one of the other guys would tell you."

For some reason, Sawyer felt deflated. "No one said anything until Zane brought it up. It's pretty obvious you avoided telling me. Why?"

Clearly annoyed, she rose from the weather-worn piece of tree trunk she'd been using as a seat. "Because it has nothing to do with you and me working together," she said stiffly.

"You didn't want me to know you were one of the Hollisters," he stated bluntly. "Why? Are you ashamed of your wealth?"

She frowned at him. "No. It's just not something I want to flaunt. For many reasons. And since you feel free to ask all these questions, I'll ask one of my own. What difference does it make to you whether I'm one of those Hollisters?"

All the difference in the world, Sawyer thought. To a man like him, it made her unreachable, or mighty close to it. Still, he wasn't a man to back down from a challenge. He couldn't allow who she was, or what she was, to change his plans.

"None, I suppose. It would have been nice, though, if you'd trusted me enough to tell me yourself."

She sighed and Sawyer thought he heard a note of regret in the simple reaction.

"I probably should've told you earlier. And if you're thinking I did it for snobbish reasons, you're wrong. I held back because I thought...well, it might make you uncomfortable." She slanted him a rueful look. "And some people believe the amount of money a person has is what makes them who they are. I guess I wanted you to see me as a person rather than a dollar sign. At least for a few days."

Making love to a woman was second nature to Sawyer. However, comforting one was a different matter. Yet the urge to hold her close and assure her that her money or social status meant nothing to him was running through him, confusing all his selfish feelings.

Ignoring the war inside his head, he stood and crossed the few short steps between them. "Viv, do I look like a man who cares about money?"

Her hazel-green gaze swept his face, then slid up and down the length of him. "Not from what I can see on the outside."

He laughed at the suspicious sound in her voice. "My grandmother and I live in the same little house I was brought into as a baby. The furniture is the same that we had when I was a teenager. She has a handful of dresses in the closet and keeps laying hens because she doesn't like store-bought eggs. I drive the same pickup truck I purchased when I first became a ranger and the only vacation I've ever had was when the agency sent me to Grand Canyon Park to observe the correct way rangers are supposed to manage crowds. But I wouldn't change a thing about my life. Money is nice. Being content is better."

A sheepish expression stole over her face. "I never thought—" She paused and shook her head. "I haven't been thinking you're an opportunist, Sawyer. I only want you to treat me like any other woman."

"That's impossible, Viv."

Her lips parted and in that moment Sawyer desperately wished the two of them had been in a more secluded spot. Rules be damned, he would've kissed her.

"Why?"

The one word was spoken huskily and Sawyer felt something raw and urgent burn the pit of his stomach.

"Because—" He reached up and caught a strand of hair

that had whipped across her cheek. As he carefully tucked it back behind her ear, he watched her eyes darken with some emotion he wanted to recognize as desire. "You're not like any other woman I've known, Viv. Not because you're from a wealthy family. But because…you're different. In the best kind of ways."

A vulnerable quiver touched her bottom lip and then she pressed them together as though she was embarrassed to admit that his closeness was affecting her in any way.

"You're different, too," she finally murmured, her voice laced with wry humor. "You're the biggest flirt I've ever met."

"I'm not flirting now. I'm stating a fact."

Clearing her throat, she stepped away from him, and it was all Sawyer could do to keep from reaching out and snatching a hold on her arm.

"Okay, I'll take that as a compliment. And we—uh, better get back to the vehicle and radio in. We might be needed."

Seeing the private moment between them was over, he picked up his thermos and followed her across the rocky slope of ground to the waiting SUV.

A few minutes later, as Vivian drove them away from the cove where they'd taken their afternoon break, Sawyer promptly picked up the radio and informed the dispatcher of their whereabouts. While he dealt with relaying the information, Vivian's thoughts were still back on the rocky shelf.

Her thoughts were consumed with every word Sawyer had said to her, every look he'd given her and the way his fingers had felt against her cheek.

His nearness had left her trembling and she hoped that ESP, or whatever he possessed, had been turned off when he'd been standing ever so close to her. Otherwise, he might have seen in her eyes just how much she wanted to wrap her arms around him and lay her cheek upon his broad chest.

Oh, Lord, she didn't know what was happening to her. She only knew she had to put a brake on these runaway feelings. Otherwise, these next six months with Sawyer were going to be fraught with drama.

"We still need to check the Javelina Trail before we leave this loop. Mort tells me there's been some vandalizing reported in that area."

Trying to shake away the troubling thoughts in her head, she glanced over at him. "That's right. Trash and beer cans left behind. Cacti hacked and rocks piled. Louis and I caught two guys building a fire on the ground about two feet away from a mesquite tree. We ticketed them and let me tell you, they were very unhappy about it."

"They're lucky you didn't have them arrested."

She shrugged. "The pair didn't have any outstanding warrants and as far as we knew that was their first offense in the park, so we decided a hefty fine would teach them a lesson."

"They could've caused a major wildfire," he said with a shake of his head. "It's crazy what some people will do. Especially when they think no one is looking."

Vivian said, "Their excuse was that they were planning to kill a rattlesnake and cook it over the fire for supper."

He laughed in disbelief. "Apparently these guys didn't understand that killing any sort of animal or reptile in the park is a major offense."

Vivian's smile had nothing to do with humor. "They understand it now."

Five minutes later, they reached the start of Javelina Trail, a two-mile trek on foot that eventually led to a pretty little valley with rock spirals and a sea of Joshua trees. In spite of making the hike hundreds of times, Vivian always looked forward to the journey and today she was even more eager to hit the trail. Being confined with Sawyer in the SUV was the same as being handed a frosted brownie and told she was forbidden to take a bite. Sheer torture.

Vivian parked the SUV in a safe, out-of-the-way spot and the two of them started up the rocky track that wound through a copse of tall saguaros and Joshua trees.

Following a few feet behind him, she determinedly pushed away the pestering thoughts of Sawyer and did her best to focus on the landscape for signs of vandalism or anything out of the ordinary.

"Bet this area gets pretty in the spring," Sawyer commented. "When everything starts blooming."

"Very," Vivian replied. "Yet for some reason this part of the park isn't visited as much as others."

"It's too far to walk from the nearest campgrounds and most folks don't want to get in the vehicle and drive unless they have to," Sawyer said thoughtfully.

"You're probably right," Vivian agreed. "But you know what, I'm not a bit sorry it's quiet back here. It's nice having the place to ourselves. Just wait till we get over to the valley. If you don't ooh and aah, then I'll know you're half dead."

Looking over his shoulder, he tossed her a grin. "I'll be sure and act impressed. I don't want you getting the idea I'm half dead."

Vivian let out a silent groan. Everything about the man was brimming with life and raw masculinity. Something she had to fight to ignore.

Thankfully, he moved on up the trail, leaving her to travel at a slower pace. After a couple of minutes, he disappeared from sight and she paused to dismantle a pile of rocks someone had made near the base of a saguaro.

"Viv! Come here! Quick!"

His urgent call had her glancing around, but she couldn't spot a sign of him anywhere.

Hurrying forward, she called out, "Sawyer? Where are you?"

Suddenly to her right, about twenty feet off the trail, the top half of Sawyer emerged above a thick stand of chaparral.

"Here, Viv." He motioned for her to join him. "We have a bit of trouble."

Vivian scurried through a maze of prickly pear and standpipe cacti until she reached Sawyer. She was about to ask him what all the fuss was about when he moved to one side to reveal a man lying sprawled on the ground.

Horrified at his battered condition, she stared in stunned fascination. "Is he alive?"

She'd barely gotten the question out when the man, who appeared somewhere in his early fifties, began to moan with pain.

Sawyer said, "Yes, but you can see he's in bad shape."

They both kneeled over the man, who was making a feeble attempt to sit up. One side of his face was swollen and colored an angry red and purple, while both eyes were little more than tiny slits. He was bleeding from the mouth and was obviously struggling mightily to talk.

"Hey, buddy, I think you need to take it easy." Sawyer purposely lowered his head back to the ground. To Vivian, he asked, "You want to stay with him while I go radio for help? Or do you want me to?"

Her mind whirling, Vivian continued to stare at the injured man. "I'll go radio headquarters and let them know we need medical help."

"Bring the first-aid kit back with you," he said. "There might be something we can do for the bleeding wounds."

She turned to hurry away, then paused to look back at him. "Sawyer?"

He glanced at her and she held up a fist and pointed to her knuckles in silent question.

He nodded in grim agreement. "Someone caused this."

Shivering at the thought, she turned and hurried away, while Sawyer's observation continued to roll over and over in her mind. *Someone caused this.* She'd heard those very same words many years ago when the ranch hands had found her father out on the range, his body beaten and broken.

Someone evil had been on this trail or could still be lurking close by. The thought made her realize just how glad she was that Sawyer was with her.

With her eyes scanning every nook and cranny of the trail for anything suspicious, she scrambled down to the SUV and radioed for help. Once she was certain the dispatcher had the correct coordinates to relay, Vivian ended the call and grabbed a small medical kit from the back of the vehicle, along with a duffle bag stuffed with an extra uniform.

When she returned to Sawyer and the injured man, she quickly offered him the duffle bag. "I thought you might pillow his head with this."

"Thanks." He stuffed the duffle bag beneath the man's head. "Are paramedics coming?"

"Yes. I gave the dispatcher our exact location and explained the situation. She was calling for help before I left the vehicle."

"Great. Maybe EMS will get here soon."

Vivian looked down at the man, who appeared to be

going in and out of consciousness. "Has he been able to say anything?"

"He muttered something about two men and money." His expression stony, Sawyer shook his head. "I'm no doctor, but this man probably has a bad concussion, maybe a skull fracture. And it appears that one ankle is broken. Possibly both."

Vivian knelt on the ground next to the man and opened the medical kit. "I'll try to clean his wounds and hopefully the paramedics won't be long in getting here."

"Did you see anyone on the way down to the SUV?" Sawyer questioned her. "Or hear anything? Like a vehicle?"

She poured peroxide onto a square cotton pad and hoped Sawyer didn't notice how her hands were trembling. "No. I didn't see or hear anything. What about you? Have you caught sight of anyone passing by on the trail?"

"No. Once he's taken care of we'll make a quick search," Sawyer told her. "I couldn't find a wallet or ID on him. I'm wondering if the attackers stole them."

Vivian began to gently wipe at the dirtied wounds on the man's face. He reacted with a low groan and then his swollen eyes cracked slightly open and attempted to focus on her.

"Who are you?" he asked in groggy confusion.

Sawyer squatted on his heels in order to be closer to the man's head. "We're Lake Pleasant park rangers. She's Ranger Hollister and I'm Ranger Whitehorse," he informed him. "Can you tell us your name?"

The man lifted fingers to his jaw and winced from the effort. "Stan Roberts. Staying with wife and kids at the campground."

"How did you get here?" Vivian asked. "We didn't see a vehicle at the trailhead."

"Walked," he answered wearily, then added, "Tell my wife—she's going to be worried."

"We'll notify her as soon as we get you out of here," Vivian assured him.

"Do you know what happened to you?" Sawyer asked him.

The nod of his head was barely discernible. "Two guys—up on the trail. They wanted money. When they found out I—" he paused and sucked in a long breath before he continued "—didn't have any—not even a phone—they went crazy and—"

"Decided to take their frustration out on you," Sawyer finished for him.

"Yeah. One stomped my ankles and told his friend I'd have hell walking out of here on broken legs. I think they might have been high on drugs or something."

Sawyer gave the victim's shoulder a comforting pat. "If they're still in the park, we'll find them. If not, the sheriff's department will."

By the time Vivian finished cleaning the wounds on his face and hands, the man was able to give them a brief description of his attackers. Unfortunately, neither she nor Sawyer recalled seeing anyone of that sort during their rounds.

"If you think you'll be okay without us for a few minutes, we're going on up the trail to look around," Sawyer told him. "We'll be in shouting distance."

The man motioned for them to go. "It's a cinch I'm not going anywhere."

Seeing the victim was as comfortable as they could make him, Vivian and Sawyer left the thorny chaparral patch, then walked through the cacti patch until they reached the trail.

As the two of them started up the hill, Sawyer said,

"Poor fellow. He's in bad shape, but it could've been much worse."

Vivian had never been a weak-willed woman. She'd never been the type to get the vapors over a broken fingernail. Yet she realized her legs were on the very verge of buckling.

She said, "He's lucky the devils didn't kill him."

"Damned lucky. You were very good back there with him," he added. "Have you ever seen anything like this here at the park before?"

Horrified that she might collapse in front of him, she struggled valiantly to gather her composure. "No. I've seen park visitors injured from falls and bites and burns and things of that sort. And I've witnessed a few heated altercations where too much beer had been consumed. But none of them were close to this extent. This is different, Sawyer. It's very…scary."

He paused and pinned her with a look of concern. "You've been a rock so far, Viv. Don't fall to pieces on me now."

She drew in a bracing breath and blew it out. "I'm not. I'm just thinking how I argued with Mort about working alone. I thought I could handle any situation. This proves I was being stupid. Furthermore, he knew it."

A faint smile touched his lips. "You could've handled this problem. Probably worse problems."

"No!" Before she could stop herself, she reached out and, wrapping both hands around his forearm, held on tight. "You're wrong about that, Sawyer. I'm so glad you're here with me. I hate to admit it, but my legs are about to buckle and—" Uncertain as to how to go on, she broke off and as her gaze connected with his, her eyes pleaded with him to understand. "I'm not nearly as strong a ranger as I thought I was."

"Oh, Viv. You are strong," he murmured, and then without warning, he wrapped his arms around her and pulled her tight against his chest.

The warm strength of his arms enveloped her, while the beat of his heart beneath her cheek soothed her like nothing else could.

Without thinking, she slipped her arms around his waist and for long, long moments, she clung to him, drawing calming sustenance from his embrace.

How much time passed while she stood there holding on to him, she couldn't say. In fact, she almost forgot the reason they were on Javelina Trail in the first place. Until she felt his fingers slipping gently through her hair and his cheek resting on the top of her head.

Shocked by how lost she'd become in his arms, she quickly stepped back. Yet even as she put several steps between them, her body, her heart, was begging her to reach for him again.

Oh, Lord, what was happening? What was she doing?

"Viv, are you okay?"

The huskily spoken question brought her gaze up to his face and the moment their eyes met, she felt something pierce the middle of her chest.

"Uh—yes, of course. I'm...sorry, Sawyer. I didn't mean to...cling to you like that. It's just that—" Shaking her head, she looked away from him, then swallowed hard. "Come on, let's go back down to the victim. We can search the rest of the trail later on."

"Right," he said. "The paramedics should be arriving soon. One of us needs to be at the trailhead to show them the way."

"I'll go down and wait for them."

She turned and started down the rocky path, only to have Sawyer catch her by the arm.

"Wait, Viv."

She paused, but couldn't bring herself to look at him. Especially with his hand wrapped so possessively around her upper arm. Just the simple touch of his fingers jolted her senses.

"What's wrong?" she asked. "Would you rather me stay with Mr. Roberts?"

"No. I...want to make sure you're all right."

She'd never be all right, she thought ruefully. Or, at the very least, never be the same now that she'd stood in the circle of his arms. But she couldn't let him know that.

"Don't worry," she assured him. "I'm not going to take the vapors on you."

His fingers eased against her flesh, then moved gently up and down her arm. Vivian knew she should step away and put a decent amount of space between them. But his touch was something she couldn't resist.

"No," he said with a dose of humor. "I don't believe you're the fainting kind. But in case you need me, my cell is in my pocket. Ring it."

Yesterday, in spite of her protest that she didn't need it, he'd given her his personal cell number. Reluctantly, she'd added it to her contact list, while promising herself she'd have to be in a dire emergency before she'd call it. Yet today it was a comfort to know she had that connection to him.

She gave him a thumbs-up and hurried on down the trail, while thinking she was growing far too close to him in far too short a time. But how on earth was she going to stop this rapid fall for the man, when everything inside her heart was pining to be near him?

Chapter Six

More than two hours later, after Stan Roberts had been hauled away in an ambulance and his wife notified, Vivian and Sawyer gave all the information they had to the local law officials, then headed back to headquarters to give Mort a detailed rundown of the incident.

"This is not the norm around here," Mort said to Sawyer. "Yes, accidents happen, but it's rare that assaults occur. I'm just glad the Christmas festivities haven't yet started. We don't want park guests to get spooked and think it's unsafe to spend the holiday with us."

"Are you going to put out bulletins advising folks to be vigilant while out on the hiking trails?" Vivian asked.

"That won't be decided until I talk to my supervisors," he told her. "It would be nice if the culprits can be apprehended. That would solve a lot of problems."

"After things settled down, Sawyer and I made the trek over to the valley, but we didn't see anything out of the ordinary over there. I doubt the creeps that jumped Mr. Roberts went that far on the trail," Vivian said to Mort.

"Viv and I showed the deputies where the altercation occurred, but they didn't find any kind of clues at the spot. Guess Mr. Roberts's descriptions are the most they have to go on. Unless they find any park visitors who might have seen a pair of suspicious characters."

Raking a hand through his rusty red hair, Mort paced around the small office for a brief moment, then paused to look at the both of them.

"Guess it's a little late in coming, but good work, you two. You handled everything right."

Not everything, Vivian thought. She'd come close to having a meltdown. If it hadn't been for Sawyer comforting her when he had, she'd probably have collapsed to the ground and sobbed uncontrollably. The uncharacteristic reaction had left her more than unsettled, it had left her doubting her ability as a ranger.

"Thank you, Mort," Sawyer said. "I may not have handled the situation like Louis, but I appreciate your praise."

He leveled a droll look at Sawyer. "While you're here at Lake Pleasant, don't be thinking you need to be like Louis. You need to be Ranger Whitehorse and nobody else. Got it?"

Sawyer grinned at the backhanded compliment. "Yes, sir. I got it."

Mort glanced at the clock on the wall. "It's only an hour before your shift ends. You two have already done enough for the day." Mort motioned them out of the office. "Go over to the cantina and have some coffee or something. I'll see you two Monday."

Outside, the two of them walked around the end of the headquarters building and across a grassy slope toward a small building where snacks and drinks were always available to rangers and park maintenance workers.

"I never imagined today to turn out like this," Vivian said as she walked alongside Sawyer.

"That's one of the things I like about being a ranger," Sawyer said. "You never know what's going to happen from one day to the next."

"So you like the unexpected," she stated. "Somehow that doesn't surprise me."

"And you don't?"

"Well, I'll put it this way. I wouldn't want every day to be this challenging."

The cantina was a dark brown building made of cinder block with a deep porch that spanned the front. A few small tables and chairs were scattered beneath the sheltered space for those who wanted to take their refreshments outside.

Sawyer opened the door, then followed Vivian into a long room furnished with utility tables and folding metal chairs.

"Wow, this is cheery." Sawyer shut the door behind him and gazed around at the Christmas decorations. "Someone has gotten into the spirit."

Vivian looked up at the gold-and-silver tinsel draped from the ceiling, the red bows fastened to the corners of the tables and a small decorated spruce standing in one corner.

"It certainly looks festive," she agreed. "And we're the only ones around to enjoy it."

He said, "The rest of the rangers are out making sure their areas are secure before the shift changes. We'd still be out, too, if we hadn't had to report to Mort."

She let out a heavy breath. "I don't know about you, but I'm glad that's over. Mort is a stickler for details. And following protocol. I think he was pleased with the way we handled things, though."

"Why wouldn't he be? We did all we could do." He pulled out a chair near the end of a table. "Here, take a seat and relax," he invited. "I'll get us something to drink. What would you like?"

She eased into the chair and after pulling off her hat, combed fingers through her tousled hair. "Coffee would be nice. If it looks fresh."

At the end of the room, he passed through a small doorway and into a kitchen area where the refreshments were stored, along with a coffee machine, microwave and refrigerator.

"From the looks of the pot, I think it's just been made," he called back to her.

"Great," she replied, while fighting the uncharacteristic urge to drop her face in her hands and weep.

After a short moment, he appeared at her side holding two foam cups and a candy bar. He placed the items on the table, then eased into a chair next to hers.

"The coffee on the left is yours. The pastries were all gone," he said, "but I found a chocolate bar. I'll halve it with you."

Smiling wanly, she shook her head. "Thanks, but the coffee will be plenty for me. You eat it."

She reached for the cup and took a careful sip of the steaming brew. It was flavored just right with cream and sugar and she darted a surprised look at him. "This is good. How did you know what I wanted in it?"

A suggestive grin spread slowly across his face and Vivian found she couldn't tear her eyes away from his lips or ignore the rapid thump of her heart.

"Yesterday you shared some from your thermos with me. I remembered how it tasted. Sweet. Like you."

Ever since she'd stepped into Sawyer's arms and laid her cheek against his chest, she'd purposely avoided making eye contact with him. She was afraid if she did, he'd be able to read all the incredible emotions she'd felt in those moments. That he would somehow see those very feelings were still stirring inside her, confusing her, yet at the same time were filling her with longing.

She forced herself to stare straight ahead at a spot on the wall. "I'm not sweet. And I'm not strong. And I'm—" Something inside her suddenly crumbled and before she could stop it, moisture was burning the back of her eyes. She blinked several times, then said in a strained voice, "I'm sorry, Sawyer."

"For what?" he asked earnestly.

Her eyes blurred with unshed tears, she turned toward him. "For being such a mess today."

"But you haven't been a mess today, Viv. You've been great."

She shook her head. "Maybe on the outside. On the inside—"

"Listen, if you're referring to that...whatever you want to call those few moments on the trail when I consoled you, then forget it. We weren't rangers then. We were just two humans."

He certainly had that right, she thought. When his arms had come around her, she'd never felt so human in her life.

"Maybe so. But I need to explain, Sawyer. When I first spotted Mr. Roberts lying on the ground behind you, I— well, it was like seeing my father all over again."

His black brows pulled together to form a look of confusion. "Your father?" he asked. "That first day we met, you told me he died from an accident."

She nodded. "That's right, I did. But actually, my family isn't sure it was an accident."

Sawyer shook his head. "Maybe you should start from the beginning," he suggested.

She released a heavy breath and sipped her coffee before she finally replied, "I happened to be home on the ranch that day. I'd taken off work to take Hannah to the doctor for a bad case of hives. We'd just gotten back home from the clinic when I heard a commotion downstairs. My mother was screaming at one of the ranch hands—something she never did. By the time I reached her, my brothers were already there trying to calm her down. When they told me the ranch hands had found Dad out on the range dead, one boot still hung in the stirrup, I was in total disbelief. Before anyone could stop me, I ran out searching for him."

"You found him," he stated flatly. "And it was bad."

Choked with painful emotions, she reached over and curled her fingers tightly over his forearm. "The cowboys had laid Dad out on the ground in front of the stables. He looked like Mr. Roberts, only hundreds of times worse. Seeing that man today, all beaten and bruised— It brought all those awful memories back to me and I...didn't handle it very well."

His hand slipped over hers and Vivian was struck by its strength and warmth. She wished she could fold her hand around his and keep holding on. But anyone could walk through the door at any moment. It would be mighty hard to explain why two rangers were holding hands.

"You said something about your family doubting it was an accident. What do they think happened?"

Extracting her hand from beneath his, she placed it safely in her lap. "Oh, it was obvious that the horse had dragged Dad for a considerable distance. But we don't know why or how the incident occurred. My little brother Joe is a deputy sheriff for Yavapai County. He's been working on the case for years now, hunting for clues and trying to patch them together. He and my brothers believe Dad was initially attacked and the dragging was a cover-up."

Sawyer whistled under his breath. "Clearly, your father was a wealthy, influential man. He might have had an enemy you didn't know about." He looked at her, his eyes full of gentle understanding. "I'm glad you told me, Viv. And about today, don't be scared. Everything will be all right. We'll be together. Right?"

Together. Yes. Strange how strongly she'd resisted the idea of having a new partner, she thought. Now, after working with Sawyer these past few days, she'd be totally lost if he suddenly up and left. What did it mean? That she was losing her common sense? Or finally letting herself be a woman again?

Wake up, Vivian! Can't you see you're falling for this flirt faster than a raindrop disappears in the desert sand? Forget about how it makes you feel to touch him. Just think about how your heart will feel once he breaks it.

Realizing he was waiting on her to answer, she quickly cleared her throat and said, "Yes, that's right. Uh—together. Until Louis comes back."

"Oh, yeah. Believe me, I haven't forgotten about Louis coming back. Obviously you haven't forgotten, either."

"No," she replied.

He tore into the candy bar and, after consuming it in four bites, rose to his feet. "I'm going after more coffee. Do you need yours warmed?"

"No, thanks. I still have enough."

He disappeared into the kitchen area, then after a moment, called to her. "Come here, Viv. I want you to see this Christmas decoration."

Curious, Vivian left her chair to join him.

"This better be good," she said, as she stepped into the small kitchen.

Grinning, he folded a hand around her arm and pulled her deeper into the tiny room. "It's more than good. Look up."

Bemused, Vivian tilted her head and then she spotted it. A green cluster of leaves tied with red ribbon was hanging from the ceiling and dangling right over their heads.

Suddenly her heart was beating hard and fast. He wouldn't dare, she thought. Or would he? "That can't be mistletoe! It looks more like sage to me. And sage doesn't count!"

Sawyer's chuckle was full of mischief and something else that sounded very much like desire.

"You know as well as I do that it's a clump of mesquite mistletoe and it definitely counts—especially with me."

She should run from the room, Vivian thought. She should run from him. But her legs refused to obey the commands of her brain. Instead, she stood rooted to the spot, scarcely able to breathe or think beyond the man standing in front of her.

Then his hands wrapped over her shoulders and his head slowly descended toward hers and she realized it was far too late to escape. Not that she wanted to. No, from the very first moment they'd met, she'd thought about having his lips on hers. His hands pulling her closer. And closer.

Sawyer. She tried to say his name, but her throat had forgotten how to work. Instead, the word whispered through her brain like a breeze teasing her skin.

By the time his lips finally settled over hers, she was already shaking, her heart beating so fast the sound of it was roaring in her ears. And then she ceased to think as everything became a delicious blur.

The taste of his hard, masculine lips was unlike anything she'd ever experienced before and as he moved them deftly over hers, she forgot about everything, except wanting him.

Unwittingly, her hands moved onto his shoulders, then slipped upward until her fingers were twining through the black hair at the back of his neck. She thought she heard him groan. Or had she been the one who'd made that needy sound? Either way, it prompted her to move closer and kiss him with reckless abandon.

It wasn't until the two of them heard the outer door of the cantina opening that they pulled apart. By then, Vivian was too dazed to move from the spot where they were standing. But Sawyer apparently had far more control over his faculties. Without saying a word, he quickly stepped around her and left the tiny kitchen.

Beyond the open doorway, she could hear him greeting another ranger and as the two men began to talk, she marveled at the casual tone of his voice. He sounded as though he'd been spending these past few minutes reading the newspaper instead of kissing her senseless.

What are you, Vivian? A silly little sophomore girl in high school? Kissing a woman senseless is all just a game to Sawyer. You need to be laughing about it. Not feeling as though the earth just tilted.

Drawing in a bracing breath, she wiped a hand over her heated face and walked out of the kitchen to join her partner.

Sawyer pushed the shovel deep into the loamy soil, turned it over, then, moving the tool a few inches over, he repeated the maneuver until a long section of ground was cultivated. Behind him, lying next to a garden rake was a pile of canna and iris bulbs waiting to be planted.

This morning he'd driven to Camp Verde and purchased the bulbs, along with new fencing material, at a farm and garden center that happened to open early on Sunday. Since he'd returned from town, he'd completed the fence repairs around the chicken coop in the backyard and was now working on a flower bed for his grandmother to enjoy this coming spring.

With only a huge bougainvillea trailing up one side of the small porch, there were no blooming flowers to brighten up the front of the little stucco house. If the flowers survived, they'd bring a bit of color to the drab yard.

He was on his knees, digging small holes for the bulbs, when Nashota stepped onto the porch and walked over to where he was working. She was still dressed in the clothes she'd worn to church earlier this morning. A long skirt made of red calico and a dark purple shirt belted at the waist. Strings of coral and turquoise beads hung from her neck. Still a beautiful woman, she looked at least ten years younger than her seventy-seven years. Yet it was the beauty and love she possessed on the inside that made her a special woman to Sawyer.

"I wondered what you were doing out here. Is that what I think it is?" she asked, eyeing the long flower bed running adjacent to the outside wall of the house.

Bracing his hands on his thighs, he looked up at her and smiled. "You weren't supposed to come outside until I finished. I wanted this to be a surprise."

She left the porch and moved across the barren yard until she was standing behind him. "I'm surprised right now. That's as good as being surprised later."

"Yellow cannas and purple irises," he said, pointing to the bulbs. "Think they'll grow with a little fertilizer and water?"

"They will if the chickens stay out of them," she answered. "And with the new fence you built this morning around the chicken coop, you've made sure the hens won't escape the backyard."

"The new fence will also make sure a coyote or stray dog doesn't snatch one or two of them," he said, flexing his shoulders to ease the growing fatigue in his muscles.

Her probing gaze studied him for long moments. "You've been working hard all day. If I didn't know better something is bothering you."

That something was five foot seven inches tall with chestnut-red hair and eyes the color of a cool, green meadow. All weekend long he'd tried to push her and that kiss in the cantina out of his mind. He'd tried not to imagine her driving her daughter and nephew to Red Bluff, or wonder who she might see once she arrived at the ranch. Maybe some cowboy there wanted to kiss her as much as Sawyer did. Maybe he was a man, who was much more suited for a ranching heiress than Sawyer could ever be.

Damn it. He was going crazy and last night had definitely proved it.

"What makes you think anything is wrong, Grandmother?"

"You're not acting like yourself. You didn't go to church with me this morning. And you came home early last night from your date."

Sawyer had avoided going to church because he'd felt sure he wouldn't be able to concentrate on the minister's sermon and having his grandmother catch him staring off in space would've been humiliating. As for his date last night—he could only describe the short outing as disastrous. Normally, on a Saturday night, he'd stay out until the wee hours of the morning. Especially when he had a pretty girl on his arm, who was willing to give him anything and everything he wanted.

But that was just the problem. He'd not wanted anything from Sherry. In fact, he'd found an excuse to end the evening practically before it got started. Even worse, he'd realized there wasn't a woman in the whole damned nightclub who'd looked attractive or interesting to him.

"Nothing is wrong, Grandmother. I guess the incident at work Friday got to me more than I thought."

"You've seen troubling things before, Sawyer."

That much was true, he thought dismally. During the years he'd worked at Dead Horse Ranch, there had been a few serious accidents and altercations. All of them had been unpleasant to deal with, but Friday's incident at Lake Pleasant had been different. Because of Vivian. Because seeing her struggling to hold on to her composure had touched him deeply.

Out on the Javelina Trail, when Sawyer had taken her into his arms, he'd desperately wanted to carry her off to a quiet place and assure her that he'd give his very life to protect her and keep her safe. The feelings had been completely foreign to him and something he was still trying to decipher in his mind.

"Yeah. It's just a part of the job," he finally responded to his grandmother. "And a ranger has to take the good with the bad."

Nashota placed a comforting hand on his shoulder. "It will take some time for you to get used to having a woman partner. But you will."

He didn't know where his grandmother's sixth sense came from, but somehow she always managed to put her finger on the very crux of the problem.

"It's an honor to be Vivian's partner, Grandmother."

"Then you should smile and be happy."

How could he be happy? For the first time in his adult life, he was terrified. In the span of a few short days, Vivian had reached inside him and touched the places he'd always believed to be safely hidden. Now thoughts of her were squeezing his heart, changing things about him that he didn't want changed.

For Nashota's sake, he forced himself to smile. "I'm always happy, Grandmother. How could I not be? I have you."

She didn't return his smile. Instead, she gave his shoulder a pat. "Finish the little garden and come inside," she told him. "I'm making coffee and fry bread."

"I'll be there in a few minutes," he promised.

She walked back into the house, and as Sawyer began to bury the bulbs, he wished he could do the same to his feelings for Vivian. But like the bulbs, he figured they wouldn't stay hidden for long. They'd soon take root and he could only wonder what would happen to him once his feelings reached full bloom.

Chapter Seven

Later that same night, Vivian had already changed into a nightgown and robe and was hanging out a uniform for work the next day when a light rap sounded on the bedroom door.

"Come in," she called, thinking her mother was going to stick her head around the door to say good-night.

Instead, Vivian looked over her shoulder to see Hannah stepping into the room.

Dressed in a pair of pink pajamas with the image of a fuzzy brown horse on the chest, her long blond hair was brushed loose against her back, while her face shined from a recent application of soap and water. She looked so sweet and innocent that Vivian almost wished she could freeze this moment in time and save her daughter from all the heartache of adulthood.

"Mom, may I talk to you for a minute?" she asked.

Vivian sat on one end of a padded vanity seat and gestured for her daughter to join her. "I always have more than a minute for you. Come sit beside me."

Hannah made herself comfortable next to her mother, then went so abnormally quiet that Vivian looked at her with concern.

"What's the matter? Are you getting sick?" She placed a hand over Hannah's forehead and was grateful to find it cool. "You and Nick rarely got off your horses. I should've made you rest more."

"I'm fine, Mom. I'm not tired at all. Nick and I had lots of fun. With all the rocks and canyons, Red Bluff is a neat place to ride. And it was nice to see Aunt Camille."

Vivian smiled faintly at the mention of her younger sister. She'd been surprised to learn that Camille had started working part-time as a waitress for a bar and grill in Dragoon. For the past year or more, she'd lived practically as a recluse, rarely ever leaving Red Bluff for any reason. With this new development, Vivian could only hope her sister was finally getting brave enough to emerge from her safe place.

"It was very nice spending time with Camille," Vivian agreed. "And we had fun helping her decorate the ranch house for Christmas, didn't we?"

"That was really fun," Hannah replied, then frowned with confusion. "I don't understand, Mom. Everybody says Aunt Camille is sad, but I think they're wrong. She smiled and laughed. You're the one who's been acting sad, Mom."

Taken aback by her daughter's comment, Vivian stared at her. "Me? I'm not sad. What gave you that idea?"

Hannah thoughtfully scrunched up her nose. "Oh, well, you've been going around with a worried look on your face. When you're not doing that you stare into space like you're thinking about something bad."

Oh, God, were her thoughts about Sawyer affecting her

so much? All weekend she'd had to fight to keep the man and his kiss off her mind. But according to her daughter's observations, she'd failed abysmally.

"I'm not thinking about bad things. Work has been very busy here lately, that's all."

Hannah persisted. "What kind of things?"

She'd not mentioned to Hannah or the rest of the family about the assault that had occurred on Javelina Trail. Having Hannah or any of her relatives worry about her safety was something Vivian always tried to avoid. Besides, the attack on the park guest was not the reason she'd been preoccupied. All weekend long she'd been mentally tormented by a dark, handsome face with a wicked smile and a kiss that had tilted her axis.

"Oh, December is a very busy month at the park. The holidays always bring more guests and that means more work for us rangers. That's all." She gave her daughter the brightest smile she could manage. "So, see, there's no need for you to be concerned about your mother."

Hannah released a dramatic sigh. "I'm glad. 'Cause I thought I was the one who'd made you sad. And I'm sorry for what I said to you the other night."

Not quite sure what Hannah was referring to, Vivian shook her head. "What are you talking about?"

Grimacing, Hannah said, "When Uncle Blake and Aunt Katherine announced the news about the baby. I said you were getting too old to give me a brother or sister. That was bad of me, Mom. I shouldn't have said that to you. Especially at the dinner table in front of the whole family."

Vivian had to admit that the remark had stung. Each year that passed with Hannah not having a father, much less brothers or sisters, caused Vivian's guilt to grow heavier. But the last thing she wanted was for her daughter to be worrying about the situation.

"It wasn't exactly nice," Vivian said bluntly, then relenting, she reached for Hannah's hand and gave it a loving squeeze. "But you're forgiven."

A smile of relief came over Hannah's face. "Thanks, Mom. And don't feel bad. It's okay if I don't ever have a brother or sister. I have Nick now and he's more like a brother than a cousin. And Little Joe will grow up someday and so will Uncle Blake and Aunt Katherine's baby. It's not like I'm all by myself."

Vivian made a thoughtful study of her daughter's face, while telling herself she wasn't envious of her brothers. She'd had her chance at love and marriage and a houseful of children. It hadn't worked out for her, but at least she had Hannah and that was a heck of a lot more than some women ever have in a lifetime.

"You're being very charitable about the whole matter," Vivian said. "Especially when you're always wishing out loud that the two of us had a family of our own."

Dropping her head in sheepish fashion, Hannah stared at the floor. "Well—Uncle Holt explained a lot of things to me and I understand better now."

Hannah's sudden change of heart was beginning to make more sense. "Oh. You've been talking to Holt? About me?"

Hannah continued to stare at the floor. "A little," she confessed. "'Cause he's your best bud and he knows what you're thinking."

It was true that she and Holt had always been close. Not that she didn't love her other siblings, but she and Holt had a special bond. No matter what occurred, or what sort of drama was playing out within the family, they always had each other's back.

However, this time Holt didn't have a clue as to what she'd been thinking about Sawyer Whitehorse. So far, she'd not hinted to her brother about the unexpected connection she was feeling to her new partner. And she had a sneaky suspicion that if Holt was aware of her emotional turmoil over the man, he'd be more than a little concerned about his sister. "So what did Holt tell you that made you so magnanimous?"

Shrugging both shoulders, Hannah lifted her head and looked at her mother. "He explained that my father broke your heart and it hasn't healed. And that some people just don't want to be married. Is that right, Mom? You don't ever want to get married?"

Ever. Never. For years she'd been telling herself she was perfectly satisfied living as a single mother. She was content to go on casual dates that meant nothing more than eating a nice meal or watching a movie. So why was Sawyer suddenly making her yearn for much more?

Seeing Hannah was waiting on a response, Vivian cleared her throat and attempted to smile. "I'm not against getting married, Hannah. But that's not something a woman does just because she wants to be a wife—or because people expect it of her. If I ever meet the right man and fall in love, then I might want to get married and have babies."

In a matter of seconds Hannah's expression changed from dubious to hopeful. "Oh. Then that means we're really going to get a whole family. Just like I've always wanted!"

Bemused by her daughter's sudden confidence, she asked, "What makes you so certain?"

A bright smile lit Hannah's face. "Mom, have you forgotten? Christmas will be here soon! And Santa will come through for me—I just know he will. I'm going to ask Santa to bring you a really neat guy. A tall, strong one, who'll make you laugh and smile. Oh, and he'll be a real hunk, too. In case you didn't know, Mom, that means very handsome. You won't be able to resist him."

Chuckling, Vivian leaned over and hugged her daughter close. "I love you, sweetie. But I'm not sure Santa delivers those kind of Christmas wishes."

Her eyes twinkling, Hannah said, "Christmas is a time for miracles. Anything can happen."

By the middle of the week, most every building and campground in the park showed signs of the coming holiday. Unfortunately, a few park visitors had been a bit too enthusiastic with overloads of lights and decorations. And it was left up to Sawyer and Vivian to get them up to safety standards without squashing their Christmas spirit.

Only minutes ago, they'd discovered an overzealous couple had strung dozens of extension cords and lights, not only on their travel trailer, but across the ground and around clumps of sage and agave plants. As if that hadn't been more than enough to issue the pair a ticket, she and Sawyer had also found an overloaded electrical strip dangling precariously from the main power outlet.

"Those folks were putting everyone in danger back there," Vivian remarked as they climbed back into the SUV to resume their patrol through the busy campground. "If some of the cords or lights had shorted and caught something on fire, the whole campground would've gone up in smoke."

This week Sawyer had taken over driving duty and each time she glanced over at him, she couldn't help but think how perfect he looked sitting in the driver's seat of the SUV. But then, he looked perfect to her no matter what the two of them were doing. Darn it.

"That's true," he said. "But come on, Viv. Park visitors are excited about Christmas coming. We don't want to ruin their holidays by writing them a ticket—unless we had to. And I didn't figure we had to this time. Did you?"

She didn't know where he'd gotten his charm, but it oozed from him like honey from a hot biscuit.

Unable to stop herself, she grinned. "No. It was an unintentional mistake on the man's part. And he was only trying to make his wife happy with all the extra lights. He won't be guilty of repeating the same offense."

Six days had passed since he'd kissed her in the cantina. Or had it been more like her kissing him? Vivian supposed that little technicality was moot. Either way, she couldn't get anything about the heated embrace out of her mind.

He let out a short laugh. "Make her happy, heck. He was trying to impress her."

"You're probably right. The woman told me they were newlyweds and this is their first Christmas together. I'm glad we didn't ruin this special time for them. Or that they didn't fry the whole campground with an electrical fire."

By now they had reached the end of the campground and he turned the vehicle onto the main road and headed north, to a group of primitive campsites they needed to check.

"How would Louis have handled those two?" he asked thoughtfully.

Surprised by his question, she looked at him. "The same way we handled it. Why?"

He shrugged. "Just wondering."

"Look, Sawyer, you're not Louis. While you're here at Lake Pleasant you need to be yourself and do things the way you think they ought to be done."

He slanted her a sly grin. "So you think I can be trusted, do you?"

Not with her heart, she thought. But that was a whole different matter. "You're a trustworthy ranger."

He looked like he was about to press her on that point, when his cell suddenly rang. After pulling the vehicle safely to the side of the road, he pulled the phone from his shirt pocket and identified the caller.

"It's Mort," he announced. "Something must be up."

Vivian watched earnestly as he swiped the phone and jammed it to his ear. It wasn't customary for Mort to call any ranger while they were on patrol. Normally, if he needed or wanted them to change their schedule, he'd simply have the dispatcher convey the message.

The conversation was brief, with Sawyer listening far more than talking. Which made it practically impossible for Vivian to pick up what they might be discussing.

"Yes, I understand," he said finally. "Thank you, sir. I'll tell her."

His expression grim, he slipped the phone back into his shirt pocket and looked at her. "I hate to tell you this, but we're in a bit of trouble, Viv."

She sat straight up in the seat, her spine ramrod stiff, and stared at him. "Trouble," she repeated, dismay transforming her voice to a raspy murmur. "For what?"

Resting his left arm on the steering wheel, he turned in the seat so that he was facing her. "I'm afraid someone saw us under the mistletoe and reported the scene to Mort."

She gasped and tried not to wilt. "Oh, hell."

"Oh, hell is right. He wasn't happy—especially with you."

A thousand scenarios rushed through Vivian's mind. None of them good. "Me!" Indignant, she stared at him. "And not you? Just what did Mort say about me?"

"That he's very disappointed you haven't kissed me again."

Her eyes widened in total disbelief and then she saw his

lips quivering with the effort to hold back a grin. Damn it, he was teasing and she'd fallen hook, line and sinker.

"Sawyer, I should bonk you over the head for that dirty trick!"

He threw back his head and laughed. "Oh, Viv, I'm sorry. I just couldn't resist."

Ever since they'd returned to work Monday morning, he'd not mentioned anything about the kiss in the cantina. And taking his cue, she'd not brought up the incident, either. Over the past few days, she'd halfway convinced herself that he'd totally forgotten the torrid embrace, or considered it nothing more than a momentary diversion.

But apparently he was remembering and that fact alone was enough to cause her heart to hammer against her rib cage.

Turning her gaze on the passenger window, she said in a strained voice, "I thought you'd probably forgotten all about that."

When he didn't immediately respond, she turned her head to see he was studying her with a look so achingly tender it was all she could do to keep from throwing herself into his arms.

"It was more than just a kiss, Viv," he said in a low voice. "That's what I remember most."

Yes, she silently agreed. It had been a heated kiss and much, much more. Still, she didn't feel comfortable admitting such to him. But then, maybe she didn't need to. Maybe every feeling wrapped around her heart was already plastered on her face.

Instinctively, the tip of her tongue came out to moisten her dry lips. "Well, it was crazy and risky," she finally replied. "And we can't let it happen again."

"You're right," he said bluntly, then grinned mischievously. "We can't let it happen again here at work. But there's always after hours."

After hours! What did that mean? Surely not that he was expecting them to have some sort of romantic rendezvous outside of work.

"That would probably be a mistake—for both of us," she said stiffly.

"Maybe for you. I don't have any direction to go, but up."

The playful lilt to his voice put a smile on her face and then before she could stop it, she chuckled. "Sawyer, you're such an idiot. But I like you. Very much."

He reached for her hand and the warm excitement rushing through her was like nothing she'd ever experienced. She didn't understand her reaction. Especially when she knew it wasn't brought on by his handsome face or long, lean sexy body or even that magical kiss. No, even when there were no words or touches igniting a spark between them, she felt an intangible connection to him.

"I like you, too. Very much."

Her gaze lifted to his face and she found herself studying his thick black lashes, the mystery of his deep brown eyes, the shallow valley beneath his nose and finally the hard curve of his lips.

I'm going to ask Santa to bring you a really neat guy. A tall, strong one, who'll make you laugh and smile.

Hannah's Christmas wish was whispering through her brain as Sawyer leaned across the console between their seats and placed his lips on hers.

The kiss was brief, but still powerful enough to cause her eyes to close and her breathing to turn shallow.

When he pulled back and settled himself behind the steering wheel, Vivian clamped her hands together and asked herself what she was going to do about him. About the wild rush of pleasure she felt each time he touched her.

Oh, Lord, it was a hopeless situation. Yet, she was incredibly happy that fate had sent him to Lake Pleasant and to her.

From the corner of her eye, she watched him put the gearshift into Drive and ease the SUV back onto the road.

"In case you hadn't noticed, there's no clump of mistletoe hanging from the headliner."

He chuckled. "I didn't need a reason to kiss you again— except that I wanted to."

His response shook her, but she tried not to show it. After all, she was six years older than him. He probably believed she was experienced with men and kisses and making love. But she wasn't. She'd only had sex with one man, and at the time, he'd been her husband. And he'd not exactly been an expert lover. Kissing Sawyer had proven that much.

Deciding they both needed to change the subject, she said, "You've not explained about Mort's call. What was the real reason?"

He smiled. "He had good news to relay to us. Sometime after midnight last night, two deputies from the Yavapai County sheriff's department arrested the guys who attacked Mr. Roberts. The pair have already confessed to the crime. He thought we ought to be the first to hear the news."

She let out a huge sigh of relief. "That is great news. So hopefully they're behind bars now and can't hurt anyone else."

"Mort made it clear that they're in jail. And because both men had warrants out for their arrest on other crimes committed in Yavapai and Maricopa Counties, they'll most likely be locked up for a long time."

"Hmm. I wonder if my brother Joe was in on the arrest," she mused aloud. "I don't know what shift he's working presently, but sometimes he has night-shift duty."

"He doesn't live on the ranch?" Sawyer asked.

"No. He's married with a baby boy. They live on his

wife's ranch, the Bar X. It's not far from the main head-quarters of Three Rivers."

"Well, I doubt he was in on the arrest. Otherwise, he would've probably already contacted you with the news."

Vivian shook her head. "I doubt it. I didn't tell any of my family about the incident on Javelina Trail. They all have enough worries of their own without adding me to the mix. Not that I was ever in any danger, but…"

Her words trailed away as she struggled to find a way to explain her situation without sounding like a real snob.

"You're from a wealthy family and they're concerned you might attract predators. Is that what you were about to say?"

The man never failed to surprise her. He seemed to instinctively understand what she was thinking and feeling. Which only made the connection between them even stronger.

"Yes. I just didn't know how to say it without making myself sound like some sort of princess, who needs protection around her at all times." She let out a cynical laugh. "Really, Sawyer, my family isn't paranoid. They only want me to be extra cautious. Because I'm a female and they think I'm gullible and vulnerable to go with it."

He looked over at her. "I don't believe you're gullible or vulnerable."

He might think differently if he knew what a loser she'd married and later divorced, Vivian thought dismally. But she'd made that mistake years ago. She wanted to believe she'd grown and changed since then.

"Thanks, Sawyer."

"And besides," he added with a wicked wink, "you now have me for a bodyguard."

She very nearly groaned out loud. "Great," she said drily. "As long as there's no mistletoe hanging around, I'll be well protected."

A half mile on down the road, he was still laughing.

Chapter Eight

That evening, as the Hollister family gathered in the den for before-dinner drinks, Holt walked up behind Vivian and slung an arm around her shoulders.

"How's it going, sis?"

She looked around and promptly gasped at the sight of his face. One eye was black and swollen, while the right corner of his bottom lip was stitched together.

"What in the heck? I hope the other guy looks worse than you," she told him.

He chuckled. "Viv, you know your little brother quit picking fights years ago. A randy colt gave me this pretty face. He thinks he's grown enough to be a stallion, but I tried to tell him he wasn't. We butted heads over the argument."

In spite of his black eye and mangled lip, she couldn't help but laugh at the comical expression on his face. Holt was one of the best horse trainers in the state and probably beyond. But over the years he'd suffered various forms of injuries. Some minor and others very serious, like a skull fracture and a shoulder torn out of its socket.

"I'm glad that's all he did to you. So what does the horse look like? I hope you didn't hurt him," she teased.

"A hell of a lot better than I do," he joked, then, squeezing her shoulders, he guided her toward a small leather couch positioned near the fireplace. "Come on, let's sit here before someone else does."

The two of them had settled themselves comfortably onto the couch when Jazelle appeared with a tray full of drinks.

Vivian quickly plucked up a margarita, but Holt took his time studying the assortment of drinks.

"What's this orange-looking thing with the brown twig in it?" he asked the housekeeper.

"It's heated punch with apple cider and a few other things Reeva adds to it. And the brown twig is a stem of cloves."

"You don't eat it, though, little brother," Vivian informed him. "It's just to add flavor."

Jazelle winked at Vivian, then said to Holt, "The drink doesn't have alcohol, so you might want to choose one that does."

"The punch will be fine," he said. "The doctor gave me something for pain when he sewed up this lip. I'd better stay away from the alcohol. Viv thinks I'm crazy enough as it is."

Jazelle was handing Holt the drink when Chandler walked up and surveyed the loaded tray.

"Have any wine there?" he asked. "I've had a hell of a day."

Holt let out a cynical snort. "I guess you think mine's been a bowl full of cherries."

"Yeah, and you got the pits instead."

"Ha. Ha," Holt retorted.

Jazelle handed Chandler a long-stemmed glass of blackberry wine, then moved across the room to where Maureen was seated with Blake and Katherine. In a far corner of the room, Hannah and Nick were busy erecting a small nativity scene on a console table.

It was a typical evening for the Hollister family, but Vivian could only wonder what Sawyer was doing right now. Having a quiet evening meal with his grandmother? Or maybe he'd stopped in Camp Verde to have dinner with a woman. The idea of him sitting across from a young, pretty woman, smiling at her, reaching for her hand and giving her a line of sweet talk bothered Vivian far more than she wanted to admit.

After sampling a sip of his drink, Chandler eased a hip onto the arm of the couch next to Vivian. "Joe tells me they arrested a pair of felons last night who'd beat up a camper at Lake Pleasant. Did you know anything about this?" he asked her.

Holt leveled a suspicious look at her. "You've been keeping something from us?"

She frowned at him. "No. Well—uh, not exactly."

"Then you didn't know anything about it?" Chandler persisted.

"Actually, Sawyer and I were the rangers who found the victim on Javelina Trail. He was in bad shape with both ankles broken. Seems as though these guys wanted to stomp the victim because he wasn't carrying any money on him."

"Oh. And that wasn't serious enough to tell your family about it?" he asked sarcastically.

"Well, gee, Holt, do you tell us everything that happens in the training pen?" she questioned crossly.

"No, but this is different," he argued. "You're a woman. You're my sister."

Vivian held a finger up to her lips and made a shushing noise. "Please, lower your voice, Holt! I don't exactly want Mom to hear this. She has enough to worry about without you adding more to the plate."

Before Holt could make any kind of retort, Chandler asked, "Who's Sawyer? I thought you always worked with Louis Garcia."

"Sorry, brothers. I'd assumed Mother had told you that Louis broke his leg. It must've slipped her mind," she explained. "He won't be able to return to work for at least six months. Sawyer was brought in as his replacement."

"So they moved him over from some other area of Lake Pleasant?" Chandler asked.

"No. Sawyer's from Dead Horse Ranch. And—" she turned a smug look on Holt "—he's young and strong and perfectly capable of seeing that no one tries to snatch me off the trail."

Holt's brows inched upward and Vivian wished she could kick herself. Exactly why had that remark come out of her mouth?

"Oh, really." He cut a sly glance at Chandler. "When was the last time we've heard Viv give a man that kind of compliment?"

Tapping a forefinger against his chin, Chandler pretended to think hard. "Hmm. I'm not sure I can remember back that far. I'd say maybe fifteen years ago."

Vivian rolled her eyes. "Just wait and see what I get you two for Christmas. Right now I'm thinking duct tape for your mouths would be perfect!"

"Okay, seriously," Holt said, "are you satisfied that you have the right guy for a partner? I mean, I've heard what all you rangers do on the job. There are times you encounter dangerous situations. You need to have someone who'll watch your back."

She didn't have to think about Sawyer being the right partner for her. Not for one second. No matter if he was a flirt. No matter that he kissed her when he shouldn't have been kissing her. She knew without a shred of doubt that he would put himself on the line to protect her. And that, in itself, was far more than Garth would've ever done for her.

"I have the right guy," she said.

Seemingly satisfied with her response, he and Chandler let the subject drop and Vivian was relieved not to have to field any more questions about Sawyer.

However, the reprieve didn't last long. During dinner, as Maureen talked about the family's upcoming Christmas festivities, she surprised Vivian by bringing up Sawyer's name again.

"Viv, since you've gotten a new partner at work, I think it would be very nice if you'd invite Sawyer to join us for dinner Saturday night," she said. "We'll be decorating the big tree in the den and most all of us will be here. I think even Joe and Tessa will be here, along with Sam. And we'd all like to meet this new man of yours."

Leave it to her mother to make it sound like she had a new boyfriend, rather than a coworker, Vivian thought.

Before Vivian could make any sort of reply, young Nick spoke up, "Don't forget Little Joe, Grandma. He'll be here, too."

"That's right," Hannah chimed right behind him, then cast a curious look at her mother. "I didn't know you had a new partner, Mom. Who is he?"

Sitting next to her, Holt shot Vivian a skeptical look. "You haven't told your daughter about Superman?"

"He's just another ranger," Vivian said to Hannah, while beneath the table, she kicked his shin.

He uttered a painful grunt, but she deliberately ignored him and turned her attention to her mother. "I'm not sure Sawyer would want to come, Mom. He might've already made plans for the weekend."

Maureen wasn't about to let her daughter slide that easily. "Well, it wouldn't hurt for you to ask. The man might appreciate the invitation. Especially since he doesn't have family of his own."

"He has his grandmother," Vivian reminded her.

"Well, I meant a wife and children."

Across the table, Hannah asked, "Is he really Superman like Uncle Holt said?"

Next to Hannah, Nick giggled. "Superman is a comic figure, Hannah. He's not real."

The girl made a face at her cousin. "I know that, silly! But he might be a super guy." She looked at her mother. "Is he, Mom?"

Oh, Lord, how did all this start? Vivian wondered. And what in the world would Sawyer think if she invited him to a family affair? Would he see the whole thing as a green light from her?

Are you stupid, Vivian? You've already kissed the man as though he was everything in the world you ever wanted. Don't you figure that was a huge green light?

Trying to block out the annoying voice in her head, she looked at her daughter. "Well, like Nick pointed out, he's not a comic figure wearing a cape. But he is nice. And he's a great ranger."

Her eyes suddenly twinkling, Hannah put down her fork and gleefully clapped her hands together. "Then please invite him, Mom. It'll be fun to have someone new around. Say you will. Please?"

Vivian felt every eye at the table turn on her. "Okay,"

she relented. "If you all feel that way, then I'll invite him. But I won't make any promises that he'll show up."

While everyone voiced their approval, Holt leaned his mouth close to Vivian's ear. "If you're half the woman I think you are, then he'll show up," he said.

If she was half the woman she wanted to be, she would've already found the courage to invite Sawyer into her home and into her life. But courage and trust were two things she'd been lacking ever since she'd learned Garth had married her for her money.

"You just take care of your face, little brother. Otherwise, Sawyer is going to think you were out on Javelina Trail."

Holt laughed, but Vivian didn't join him. She was too busy wondering how Sawyer was going to react when she invited him here to Three Rivers.

On the other hand, meeting Hannah and the rest of her family might be the very best thing for both of them, Vivian decided. Seeing that she was all about family would make it clear that she wasn't the kind of woman who'd be content to have a heated affair with him, or any man.

The next afternoon, Sawyer and Vivian, along with two other rangers, were asked to help erect a portable stage where a Christmas candle lighting and caroling service was scheduled to be held on Sunday night.

With the sunny weather much warmer than usual, putting the heavy pieces of plywood together turned out to be a sweaty job. By the time it was completed, Sawyer was more than ready to head to the cantina for a cool drink.

"Let's sit out on the porch," Vivian suggested. "There's a cool breeze."

Sawyer leveled a knowing grin at her. "Afraid of the mesquite mistletoe hanging in the kitchen?"

She pulled a playful face at him, then gestured to a table at the far end of the porch. "You go sit," she told him. "I'll get our drinks."

Chuckling, he shook his head. "All right, fraidy-cat. You go sit. I'll get our drinks. Something tall with plenty of ice."

By the time he'd returned a couple of minutes later, she had pulled off her hat and combed fingers through her hair. The long sleeves of her shirt were rolled up on her arms to give him a view of smooth pale skin and toned muscles.

"Sweet iced tea with lemon," he announced as he set the tall foam glass in front of her. "With a straw."

She gathered the drink with both hands and took a long sip. "How did you know I wanted a straw?"

"Because most women like them."

She rolled her eyes, but he could see she was trying hard not to smile. "I'm not most women."

He would certainly agree with that statement. After nearly two weeks of working side by side with the woman, he still couldn't figure out exactly what was making him so attracted to her. Sure, she was pretty and she had a damned good body. But he'd dated plenty of women with pretty features and alluring curves before. Yet none of them made him feel like Vivian made him feel. It didn't make sense.

"Yes, I'm learning that."

She didn't reply and he used the silence to down a portion of his soda.

After a moment he said, "Mort asked if I'd be willing to work Sunday night. He says with all the Christmas activities going on the park will be flooded with guests. I told him no problem. I could be here. Did he ask you?"

"Yes, he mentioned it to me yesterday and I told him I could be here. I don't mind working and the caroling is enjoyable. I'm looking forward to it."

She turned her gaze on the short lawn in front of the cantina, then drummed her fingers lightly on the tabletop. Sawyer got the impression she was nervous about something, he just couldn't imagine what might be causing her to be on edge. If he'd done something to upset her, she wouldn't be bashful about telling him.

"Is anything wrong, Viv?"

She looked at him, and for one brief second he thought he saw a sad shadow pass across her face. But then she smiled and like all the other times she'd smiled at him, he felt like she was handing him the moon and the stars and everything in between.

"No. Not at all. I— Actually I have something to ask you."

"And that makes you nervous?" he asked with faint surprise. "You should know you can ask me anything."

Her lips took on a wry slant. "Well, it's been a long time since I've done anything like this. And I feel rather awkward."

He'd thought she was going to question him about something here at work. Now he wasn't so sure.

In an effort to lighten her mood, he teased, "Maybe if we went inside and stood beneath the mistletoe you'd lose that awkward feeling."

She rolled her eyes at him. "Stop it! We're not going to talk about that damned mistletoe anymore. Or kissing or anything close to it! I'm the mother of a twelve-year-old. I'm six years old than you. Doesn't that mean anything to you?"

With any other woman it probably would make him back away, Sawyer silently admitted. But with Vivian those credentials only made her sexier.

"Should it?" he asked.

A grimace flattened her lips. "I'm sure you flirt with plenty of older divorcees, who also have children."

Normally the sarcasm in her voice would have amused him, but not today. He was beginning to realize that he wanted her to take him seriously as a man. One that desired her more than she could possibly guess. The idea was a scary one for Sawyer. Especially when he'd always been bound and determined never to couple the words *serious* and *woman* in the same sentence.

"You're the only older divorcee I know who also happens to be a mother."

"Exactly my point. I'm not your type. Nothing about me is your type."

How could she possibly know the type of woman he preferred? She'd never met any of his dates. "Has someone been telling you about my past girlfriends?"

"Past? Oh, Sawyer. Sometimes you are so funny."

To his amazement, he felt a flush of embarrassed heat crawling up his neck. "Okay, so I'm not a monk. I have some past girlfriends and some that are more recent."

She sipped her tea, then waved away his words. "No matter. How many women you date is none of my business."

But Sawyer wanted it to be her business. And that made no sense at all. "Okay, so what did you want to ask me?"

She glanced around as though she was checking to make sure they were alone, then leaned slightly toward him. "I want to invite you to Three Rivers for dinner on Saturday night—uh, that's tomorrow night. Most of the family will be there and we'll be trimming the Christmas tree afterward. It's always a fun time."

Sawyer was totally stunned. Go to Three Rivers Ranch and meet her family? This was not even close to what he'd been expecting.

"Are you serious?"

His doubt put a frown on her face. "Completely serious. Why wouldn't I be?"

He was about to answer when several rangers suddenly emerged around the corner of the headquarters building and approached the porch of the cantina. His buddy Zane was among the group and as soon as he spotted Sawyer and Vivian, he headed straight toward them.

Ambling up to their table, his grin encompassed both Sawyer and Vivian. "Hey, you two. How's your day been going?"

"Couldn't be better," Vivian answered. "We just finished putting the stage together for the caroling. Now all it needs is decorations. Are you good at decorating?"

Chuckling, Zane gestured to Sawyer. "He's the man for that job."

"Thanks for volunteering me," Sawyer managed to retort, while three-fourths of his brain continued to spin wildly with Vivian's invitation. What did it mean?

Frowning, Zane bent forward to peer closer at Sawyer's face. "What the heck, buddy? Are you feeling okay? You look like you've just seen a ghost."

No. He wasn't seeing a ghost, Sawyer thought. He was seeing an end to all the things that had once made him happy. Damn it, how could a woman rearrange a man's thinking in so little time?

"I'm fine and I'll be even better when you get the heck out of my face."

Zane looked at Vivian and winked. "I know how to take a hint. Sorry you're saddled with such a crab for a partner," he said to her. "Maybe you can talk Mort into sending you over to our side of the park."

"Thanks, but I can handle Sawyer's crabbiness."

Laughing loudly, Zane slapped Sawyer's shoulder. "See you later, buddy."

Sawyer acknowledged his friend by lifting a hand in farewell. Across the table, Vivian was studying him closely.

"You do look a little pale," she said. "And you were rather short with Zane. Are you feeling all right?"

"Zane doesn't take me seriously. Besides, he has a tough hide. I'm just a bit hungry, that's all."

"I'll go inside and get you a pastry or candy bar," she said. "You just sit and relax."

She started to rise from her chair, but Sawyer swiftly reached across the table and caught her by the hand. "No. I'll get something later," he told her. "I'm—uh, I'm still thinking about your invitation. I'm having a little trouble understanding you—why you want me at a family function. Ever since we first met you've been pointing out that we're mismatched."

Her gaze dropped pointedly to where his hand had trapped hers against the tabletop, but Sawyer wasn't ready to let go. Not yet. Not when her little hand felt so warm and soft in his.

"We're not mismatched as work partners," she corrected him. "I think we're perfect together."

Perfect would be her completely naked, lying next to him in a big soft bed, he thought, as he rubbed his thumb over the back of her hand.

"I'm not talking about work partners," he murmured.

She eased her hand from his and drew in a deep breath. "Look, Sawyer, the two of us spend our days together. You're important to me so that makes you important to my family. They'd like to meet you and I had hoped you would want to meet them. But if you'd rather not, just say so. I'll understand."

You're important to me. He never wanted to hear a woman say those words to him. Unless it had been from his mother when he'd been a very small child and hungry for affection. But Onida had never said such a thing to him. And now—well, it was hard for him to believe he was special to Vivian.

"Hmm. So it's as simple as that, is it?"

She looked away from him and Sawyer watched her throat move as she swallowed.

"Yes. As simple as that."

Sawyer was hardly convinced, but decided her motive for the invitation no longer mattered. There was no way in hell he could turn down the chance to spend time with Vivian away from work, where they could be just a man and woman together.

"Then I'd be very happy to accept your invitation," he told her. "What time should I be there?"

"We have drinks around six and dinner around seven," she said. "Why don't you come around five? That way I can show you around the ranch a bit before everyone starts to gather. Oh, and my brothers will be wearing jeans, so don't bother dressing up."

"Sounds good."

The smile that suddenly appeared on her face turned his insides to warm mush and made him forget about the doubts and insecurities he harbored about losing his heart to a woman like Vivian.

"It will be good," she promised.

The next evening, a few minutes before five, Vivian stood in front of her vanity mirror and cast a critical eye at her reflection.

Sawyer had never seen her in anything but the uniform they were required to wear for work. What was he going to think when he saw her like this? That she'd dressed up just to impress him?

The red-and-green circle skirt hit her midcalf and swirled against her brown suede boots. The red, long-sleeved sweater she'd chosen to pair with the skirt hugged her upper body and turned her wavy chestnut hair to the color of flames.

Had she overdone it? And why was she even worrying about her appearance?

A knock on the bedroom door put her self-directed question on pause.

"Come in," she called.

As she picked up a hairbrush from the vanity, she caught the reflection of Hannah entering the room.

"Wow, Mom! You look awesome!" she exclaimed.

Her daughter's enthusiastic compliment eased Vivian's doubts somewhat, but not completely. "You think so?"

"Oh, yeah, Mom. You're beautiful!"

Turning slightly, she bent and placed a kiss on Hannah's cheeks. "You look very pretty, too, honey."

Forgoing her cowgirl gear for one evening, Hannah was wearing a pair of skinny jeans and a white cable-knit sweater. A headband adorned with glittery reindeer antlers held her long blond hair back from her face.

Hannah glanced down at herself. "Grandma bought these ballerina flats for me when she went to Prescott the other day. I thought it would make her happy if I wore them tonight instead of my cowboy boots."

Vivian eyed the red shoes with faux jewels on the toes. "Those are perfect for Christmas. I'm sure Sawyer is going to think I have a beautiful daughter."

Hannah tilted her head quizzically to one side. "Mom, are you having a date tonight?"

Vivian studied her daughter's curious expression, while

thinking a part of her did consider this night to be a date of sorts. Yet she didn't want to admit it to herself or to anyone else, especially her daughter. Not when it was as clear as day that all she and Sawyer could ever be were friends and coworkers.

"Why no," she said, purposely making her voice light and cheery. "This is just having a friend join us for dinner, that's all."

Hannah looked crestfallen. "Oh, that's a bummer. I thought maybe this guy was somebody you really liked."

"Well, I do really like Sawyer. I'm just not sure it's in the same way you're thinking."

Hannah sat down on the vanity seat and picked up a tube of lipstick. "I'm thinking you never invited any of your coworkers to Three Rivers before. So this guy must be special. That's what I'm thinking."

It did look that way, Vivian realized. Even Sawyer had thought so. But then, she figured he'd never met a woman who could resist him.

"Your grandmother is the one who insisted I invite Sawyer," Vivian pointed out. "It wasn't my idea."

Hannah opened the lipstick and held it up for Vivian to see. "May I wear some of this tonight? Please. It's Christmas and I want to look pretty!"

"It's not Christmas yet. And you already look pretty. But—" She picked up a different tube of lipstick and handed it to her daughter. "You may wear this shade. But don't plaster it on. Just dab it."

"Oh! That's so pale. I want red like yours!"

"When you get a few years older you may wear red." Vivian softened her reply with a gentle smile. "For tonight you're going to look like a proper young lady."

Seeing her argument was going nowhere, Hannah

handed the pale pink lipstick to her mother. "Okay, you win, Mom. Will you put it on for me?"

Vivian was applying a sheer layer of color to Hannah's lips when the landline phone on the nightstand rang. Knowing it was most likely someone from downstairs, she finished with Hannah's lipstick then picked up the receiver.

Before she could say hello, her mother's voice sounded in her ear. "You might want to hurry on down. Your guest is coming up the drive."

"Oh! I'll be right there."

She dropped the phone on its hook and hurried toward the door. "Sawyer's here. I'm going outside to meet him."

Hannah hopped to her feet. "I'm coming, too!"

Vivian paused long enough for Hannah to catch up with her, then grabbed her daughter's hand as the two of them rushed through the house and out the front gate.

As they stood waiting for Sawyer to park his truck, Hannah looked up at her and grinned.

"Mom, you're acting like Santa is coming to give us a bunch of gifts."

All day, she'd been trying to contain her excitement at having Sawyer here on the ranch. But now that he'd actually arrived, Vivian felt practically giddy.

"Santa Claus doesn't wear blue jeans."

Hannah's eyes twinkled. "This one might."

Sawyer as Santa? No. He wasn't the daddy type, much less the Santa type. But he had already given her a special gift. He'd made her feel like a woman again.

Chapter Nine

For the past few miles since Sawyer had passed a sign reading Bar X Ranch, the fencing along both sides of the narrow dirt road had changed to that of pipe painted a pristine white. Once he'd finally turned into the Three Rivers entrance, he'd expected a Western-style mansion to soon come into view. Instead, he drove another two miles when he topped a rocky rise and found himself gazing at the Hollister homestead spread across a wide, desert valley.

As he drew closer, he could see the large three-story house was painted white and trimmed with black. Most of the structure was shaded by massive cottonwoods, along with smaller mesquite trees. A considerable distance to the right of the house, an enormous work yard consisted of several barns large enough to serve as airplane hangars, a few smaller utility sheds and a network of holding pens.

The road coming into the ranch circled beneath a stand of cottonwoods to pass directly in front of the house. Uncertain as to where he should park, Sawyer eased his truck to a stop a few feet away from a gate leading into the front yard.

By the time he'd killed the motor and climbed to the ground, he spotted Vivian and a young girl hurrying down the walkway toward him.

Smiling, Vivian waved at him and Sawyer lifted a hand in acknowledgment as he walked across the drive to meet her.

"I see you made it," she said as the three of them met at the yard gate. "Did you have any trouble finding the place?"

"No. The directions you gave me were easy to follow." He could hardly tear his eyes off Vivian, but out of courtesy he turned his attention to the girl hanging on to Vivian's arm. "You must be Hannah," he said. "I'm Sawyer Whitehorse."

The girl looked from him to Vivian, then back to him before she smiled and offered her hand to him. "You're right, I'm Hannah. Welcome to Three Rivers, Mr. Whitehorse."

Smiling at the charming child, he shook her hand and said, "Thank you, Hannah. And I'd like it very much if you'd call me Sawyer, okay?"

"Sure. That would make me happy, too!"

"Well, now that you two have introduced yourselves to each other, what would you like to do?" Vivian asked Sawyer. "We can go in and wait for everybody to gather in the den. Or we can go to the ranch yard and show you around."

"Oh, yeah, Sawyer! You'll like the ranch yard. I'll show you my horse and saddle!" Hannah exclaimed. "And we have a bunch of new yearlings. Our mares were really busy this spring!"

Clearing her throat, Vivian glanced helplessly at Sawyer. "She's all ranch girl."

"Well, I'm all for Hannah's idea," Sawyer said, instinctively knowing already that he and Hannah were going to be friends. "I'd love to see the horses."

"Yippee!"

Hannah started to race off ahead of them, then suddenly put on the brakes. "I forgot. I need to go get Nick. His feelings will be hurt if he doesn't get to go."

"That's right," Vivian told her. "Go get Nick. Sawyer and I will walk slowly and you two can catch up with us."

"Right!"

Hannah took off in a rush toward the house and Vivian smiled up at him. He couldn't believe how gorgeous she looked this evening. And it wasn't just the pretty skirt that draped over her hips, or the sweater that outlined the shape of her breasts. No, it was the sparkle in her green eyes, the way her red lips made her white teeth gleam and the way her shiny hair dipped in an alluring wave against her cheek. This evening she didn't look like a ranger. She looked all woman.

"Thank you for being so patient with my daughter," she told him. "Hannah loves the ranch and everything that goes with it. And she never meets a stranger. Just try not to let her talk your ear off."

"Don't worry. I have friends on the reservation who have kids. I know what they're like. Besides, you and I were Hannah's age once."

Smiling, she looped her arm through his and turned him toward the ranch yard. "Let's head on," she suggested. "We don't have much daylight left."

As they walked along, he glanced down at her. "You look very beautiful tonight. You make me feel dowdy in these old jeans."

"Those jeans are exactly the kind I'm used to seeing my brothers wear to the dinner table. You look very nice. Not like a park ranger at all."

He laughed. "I was thinking the same thing about you."

She laughed with him and then gestured ahead to where several ranch hands were spreading feed and hay to a herd of cows and calves.

"That's a small herd Blake purchased the first of the week from a Prescott rancher. He and Matthew like to keep them quarantined for a few days before they turn them out to pasture. Just in case they develop shipping fever or anything like that."

The herd she was calling small would probably add up to a hundred or more head and would cost a fortune to someone like Sawyer.

"I recall that Blake is your brother—the one who's going to have the new baby. And Matthew is?" he asked, while relishing the feel of her hand on his arm. She smelled sweet and spicy, like a cookie just begging to be bit into, and with each step he could feel the side of her hip brushing against his.

"Yes, Blake is my oldest brother and the manager of Three Rivers. Matt is the foreman and has held that position since before Dad died. When he first came to work for us, he was newly married. But they divorced soon afterward. Not every woman is cut out for ranch life," she added.

He slanted her a wry look. "Not every woman is cut out for life on the reservation, either. But some thrive there. Like my grandmother. I liken her to *castilleja,* or prairiefire, as she calls Indian paintbrush. It roots down and remains strong and beautiful while surviving the harshest soils and elements."

"I hope to meet her one of these days," Vivian said,

then added jokingly, "I want to ask her a few questions about her grandson."

Sawyer chuckled. "I have her totally fooled. She thinks I'm the grandest thing since the invention of matches."

She started to reply, when the sound of running foot-steps approaching from behind distracted her. Sawyer glanced over his shoulder to see Hannah and a brown-haired boy close to the same age rushing up to them.

"We're here!" Hannah exclaimed. "And we're ready to give Sawyer a grand tour of the ranch yard."

"Don't you think you should introduce Nick first?" Vivian prompted.

"Oh, sure." She nudged the boy forward. "Sawyer, this is Nick Hollister. We're cousins. And best friends. Right, Nick?"

He grinned at Hannah. "The best," he answered, then turned his attention to Sawyer. "I'm pleased to meet you, Mr. Whitehorse."

Like Hannah, Nick extended his hand to him and Saw-yer realized the Hollister children had certainly been taught their manners. "Hannah is going to call me Saw-yer so I think you should, too," he told the boy.

"Yes, sir," Nick said, "I mean, Sawyer."

With the introduction out of the way, Vivian asked, "So what would you like to look at first?"

"The yearlings!" Hannah practically shouted, while Nick chimed at the same time, "The mares' paddock!"

Chuckling, Vivian once again reached for Sawyer's arm and he gladly gave it to her. It didn't matter if they had two young chaperones tagging along. Being with Vivian like this was a sweet pleasure and nothing like he'd ever experienced before. Was this a glimpse of what it was like to be a real family man?

Damn, was he cracking up? Even if he had only been

a little kid, he'd not forgotten what it was like with his parents. The fussing and fighting between them, the resentment and spite that had permeated every room in the house. There had been no love and very little toleration.

But he wasn't his father, Sawyer assuredly reminded himself. He wasn't going to trust his heart to the wrong woman. No. He might never trust his heart to any woman.

Vivian shouldn't be this happy. To have Sawyer standing by her side, interacting with the children and viewing everything about her home as though it was as important to him as it was to her, shouldn't be thrilling her this much, but she had to admit that it was.

"It's getting dark. We'd better get back to the house before Mom sends out a search crew for us," Vivian announced when they emerged from the foaling barn.

"But there's still the barn where Uncle Chandler doctors the animals," Nick spoke up. "Sawyer hasn't been there yet. And I want him to see the raccoon that Uncle Chandler has been making well."

"Yeah! He's so cute." Hannah seconded Nick's idea.

"Sorry, kids," Vivian said. "We'll have to do that the next time Sawyer comes for a visit. We don't want to make dinner late."

As the four of them started walking in the direction of the house, Sawyer arched a questioning brow at Vivian. "Where did a raccoon come from? Is it a pet?"

She shook her head. "Some of the ranch hands found the wounded animal out on the range. Its foot was mangled, so they brought it in to Chandler. My brother never turns away any kind of animal that's injured or sick. Like someone else I happen to know," she added.

Only a couple of days ago, she and Sawyer had found a wounded hawk near a hiking trail. He'd carefully managed to cage the bird without causing it any more harm, and they'd hauled it into a wildlife conservatory to be nursed back to health.

"Sometimes animals need our helping hand," he said.

"Sometimes we humans need them, too," she replied.

He glanced at her and just for a moment she thought she spotted a flash of vulnerability in his eyes. But then he grinned and it all disappeared behind a mischievous twinkle.

"Yeah. Even guys like me."

Everything Sawyer had expected the Three Rivers ranch house to be turned out to be all wrong. Instead of opulent rooms with furniture too nice to be touched, much less used, the large house was warm and homey and very comfortable. The Hollister family was equally inviting, and by the time dinner was over and everyone had gathered in the den to trim the tree, he felt as though he knew them well.

The first thing he'd gathered about Vivian's brothers was that the men were all rugged, down-to-earth guys, who respected their mother and the land that made their living. Blake appeared to be the quiet, serious one of the bunch, except for when his pretty wife was at his side. Chandler possessed a laid-back personality, while Holt was the jokester of the group. Joseph, the deputy and family man, seemed to be a younger version of his brother Blake.

However, it was Vivian's mother, Maureen, who really caught Sawyer's attention. Wearing a festive skirt and blouse, she looked attractive and feminine, especially for a woman of her age. Yet when he noticed Maureen's hands, he could see they were strong and weather-worn with short unpolished nails. Vivian had told him that her mother was an outdoor woman, who wasn't afraid to do a man's job. At the time, he'd doubted her. After all, why would a woman of Maureen's wealth and social standing be doing hands-on ranch work? But tonight, he could see for himself that the Hollister matriarch was like her daughter, far from a typical woman.

"Looks like Viv is busy. Mind if I have a seat?"

Sawyer looked up to see Sam, the older man who'd been introduced as Joseph and Tessa's ranch foreman, gesturing to an empty cushion on the couch. He was cradling a squatty glass filled with bourbon and ice, most likely his second or third for the evening, yet he appeared perfectly sober. Just from looking at his wiry body and leathery face, Sawyer figured he had the constitution of a bull.

"Sure," Sawyer told him. "I think it's going to take Viv and Katherine a while to untangle that box of Christmas tree lights."

"You don't want to help?" Sam asked.

Sawyer did want to help, but he didn't want to intrude on a family moment. "Maybe later. When they get to the easy stuff."

"This your first time coming to Three Rivers?" Sam asked.

Sawyer nodded. "I live on the reservation up near Camp Verde. I'd heard of this ranch before but never seen it until this evening."

Sam cackled. "Son, it would take you days to see all this ranch. Seven hundred thousand acres is a lot of land." His eyes narrowed thoughtfully on Sawyer's face. "You say your name is Whitehorse?"

"That's right. Do you know anyone by that name?"

The old man rubbed a thumb and forefinger against his whiskered chin. "I used to. He rode bareback broncs on the Indian Rodeo Circuit. Name was Willy Whitehorse."

Sawyer looked at him with surprise. "He was my uncle.

I have a few of the buckles he won. That was years ago, though."

"Yeah, a long time back I heard he died."

Sawyer nodded, while thinking of the uncle he'd lost only a few short years after his father had passed. At one time he had idolized Willy and had wanted to try his hand at riding broncs, too. But his uncle had rightly discouraged him by pointing out that Sawyer was simply too tall to be successful at the sport.

"He had a stroke and died suddenly," Sawyer told him.

"That's too bad. I liked him. He was a happy guy always telling jokes." He sipped the bourbon, then cast another curious eye at Sawyer. "Maureen tells me you're a park ranger like Viv."

Sawyer nodded. "Viv and I work together."

Sam shot him a pointed grin. "Bet that's lots of fun."

He'd not expected that kind of reply to come out of the old man's mouth. "You say that like you know what it's like to work with a woman."

"Sure, I know what it's like. Me and Tessa work together all the time on the Bar X. She's dainty-looking, but she's a real cowgirl. Course, she'll probably be hanging up her spurs for a while if she and Joe decide to have another youngin' to go with Little Joe."

Yes, Sawyer could see the Hollister bunch was all about family. Was that why Vivian had invited him to dinner tonight? To show him exactly how far apart the two of them really were?

No. He didn't want to ponder those questions now. Tonight was too special to ruin it with thoughts about the future. When he'd be back at Dead Horse Ranch and Vivian would be out of his life.

For the next quarter hour, he visited with the old foreman, until Vivian walked over to where the two men were sitting and reached for Sawyer's hand.

"Come on, lazy," she said. "We have the lights untangled and you're just the man to help us put them on the tree."

Sam motioned for Sawyer to get to his feet. "Better go, son. We have to keep the womenfolk happy. Especially at Christmastime."

Laughing, Vivian winked at Sawyer. "You need to listen to Sam. He's an expert on women."

"That's good to know," Sawyer said as he rose from the couch. "I'll be sure to get his phone number before I leave."

Sam laughed and sipped his bourbon.

Nearly an hour and a half later, the twelve-foot blue spruce was loaded with lights and ornaments and silver-and-gold tinsel.

With Hannah and Nick oohing and aahing over the tree, Vivian stepped back to admire the effort they'd put into placing the decorations in just the right spot.

"I think this tree is the prettiest we've ever had," she declared.

"I like the star on top," Tessa spoke up as she jostled Little Joe on her hip. "The Christmas star guided the Wise Men and shepherds to the manger in Bethlehem. Maybe this star will guide happiness to our family."

Vivian kissed her sister-in-law's cheek, then pecked another on the top of her baby nephew's head.

"I so hope you're right," she said, then moved a few steps over to where Sawyer was standing next to Maureen.

"I'm going to apologize for my daughter," Maureen said to him. "She should have warned you that she was going to put you to work tonight."

He smiled at her and Vivian was amazed at how comfortable he seemed to be around her family. She'd not expected that any more than she'd expected for this night to fill her with such joy.

"I'm used to it," he joked.

Maureen chuckled, then directed a glance at Vivian. "Matt built a fire a few minutes ago on the patio. Why don't you take Sawyer out for a break? He deserves it after all this tree-trimming commotion."

As best as Vivian could tell, everyone was inside the den. That meant she and Sawyer would be alone. Was her mother actually trying to throw the two of them together?

Either way, Vivian wasn't about to argue the matter. Since Sawyer had arrived, she'd not had one private moment with him.

"Good idea," she said to her mother, then turned to Sawyer. "Come on. I'll show you out back where we can get some fresh air."

He followed her to the opposite side of the den, where a pair of French doors opened onto the patio and as they stepped outside, Vivian tried not to wonder what the rest of the family were thinking about her and Sawyer's exit.

They probably aren't thinking anything, Vivian. You and Sawyer are alone together every day. A few minutes on the patio isn't any different.

Maybe it wasn't, Vivian argued with the pestering voice in her head. But it sure didn't feel the same. Her heart was tap dancing against her ribs and her mouth was so dry she couldn't begin to swallow down the nervous lump in her throat.

Standing next to her, Sawyer gazed at the twinkling icicle lights bordering the eaves of the patio roof. "Now this looks like Christmas is coming. Someone spent a few hours putting up these lights."

"A couple of ranch hands did this handiwork," Vivian

told him. "Hannah and Nick wanted to make sure Santa could find the back entrance to the house. Just in case he doesn't want to come through the front door."

He gestured to a spot out on the lawn where a group of lighted reindeer were pulling a sleigh. "I suppose that's in case Santa's reindeer play out and he needs to make a change."

Vivian laughed. "Right. Having children around at Christmas makes the celebrating more fun."

They stepped onto the covered patio and instinctively gravitated toward the rock firepit where low flames were radiating waves of heat.

"This is where we spend most of our time in the warmer months. Mom likes to have barbecues," she explained. "And we all like eating outdoors."

"This is nice," he said, then added with a wry chuckle, "and quiet."

Her little laugh sounded more like a gasp for air and she berated herself for having such a schoolgirl reaction to him. Just because they were alone in the dark, didn't mean he was going to make romantic advances. Especially after she'd made a point of telling him she wanted him to keep his hands to himself. But did he really believe that's what she actually wanted? How could he? She didn't even believe it herself.

"I have to apologize for Holt. He likes the Christmas music loud. Blake turns it down, but Holt comes along and punches the volume back to high."

She took a seat on the wide stonework that circled the fire and Sawyer eased down next to her.

"You don't have to apologize for anything, Viv. I've enjoyed everything about this evening. Even the music. Your family is great. And not at all what I expected them to be."

Her gaze lifted and for a moment she watched orange-and-golden hues of light from the fire flickering across his face. He looked so young and strong and sexy. She'd be crazy to think she could hold his attention for more than a very short time.

She asked, "What were you expecting? Stiff businessmen in suits sitting around counting stacks of money? And my mother overseeing everything from a throne?"

He chuckled. "Not exactly. I guess—well, I wasn't expecting all of them to be so friendly with me. But I suspect they're all being nice for your sake."

Vivian couldn't help herself. She reached over and wrapped both her hands around his. "Don't kid yourself. You'd know right off if they didn't like you. And I can tell you've made a big hit with Hannah and Nick."

"Your daughter is very special. And so is Nick. To be honest, Hannah surprised me, too," he admitted.

"Really? In what way?"

"Kids can be possessive of their parents. Especially when there's just one. I thought she might resent you giving me attention."

Or might resent the idea of her mother having a boyfriend? Was that what he'd actually been thinking? No. Their relationship wasn't anything of the sort, she reminded herself. It couldn't be. Not at work. Or anywhere else. He wasn't in the market for a wife, or a ready-made family.

With that thought in mind, she realized she should let go of his hand, but she couldn't make herself release her hold on him. Touching him made her feel alive and good and happy. It was that simple.

"Thankfully Hannah doesn't have that sort of nature. She's very sharing and generous, especially with the people she loves. That's not to say she's perfect. I do have my problems with her. Mostly when it comes to horses and saddles. She wants every one of them she sees. But I want her to understand that she can't have everything she wants—even though we do have enough money to buy it."

"She doesn't come across to me as spoiled."

"Thanks. I do work at keeping her that way." Sighing, she forced her hands away from his and held them out to the fire to compensate for the loss. "You see, right after Hannah was born Dad created a trust fund for her. She won't be able to touch the money until she starts college, so before that happens I want her to learn to be responsible and not confuse her wants with her needs."

He nodded. "That's understandable. Most of us tend to do that on occasion. Except for my grandmother. She's always content to have only the essentials. However, most young people nowadays have different ideas about money. And everything else."

Vivian groaned. "*Everything* is the key word there."

His questioning gaze slipped over her face and she wondered what he was really thinking about her now after he'd seen her at home, with family.

"It would be helpful if Hannah's father was close by to help you with her upbringing. Does he see her very often?"

Surprised by his question, she asked, "Have you forgotten? I told you I've not seen Garth in eleven years."

Frowning, he shook his head. "I remember. But that's between you and your ex. Surely Hannah sees her father on a regular basis."

Vivian couldn't stop the short, cynical laugh that burst past her lips. "Other than showing her a handful of photos and telling her what we can about the man, Hannah doesn't know her father. We divorced shortly after she was born. And once he hightailed it from the ranch, we've never heard from him again."

* * *

Amazed, Sawyer stared at her. "You mean he just left the area and never contacted you again? I don't understand. What about his baby? His daughter?"

Her features suddenly changed to a stark, unfeeling mask. "Garth held no feelings whatsoever for Hannah. In fact, when I told him I was divorcing him, he was relieved that I wasn't going to make demands on him to be a father."

"Meaning you didn't ask for child support?"

"I didn't want to go through the constant fight of trying to collect. At that time, Garth was between jobs. He had no income of his own. You see, he married me thinking the Hollister wealth would take care of him for the rest of his life. When he discovered he'd have to work to support himself and his wife, our marriage went on a fast, downhill slide."

Since Sawyer had met Vivian, he'd often wondered what had occurred to end her marriage. Now that she was actually telling him, it was difficult to believe that a man could walk away from her and the child they'd created together. But there were plenty of fools in the world and it appeared as though she'd been married to one.

He must have been quietly digesting her information far longer than he'd thought, because she said, "Now you're thinking I'm an idiot for marrying the jerk in the first place. And I'll admit it, I must have been an idiot. I was too blind to see what he was all about. It wasn't until after we were married I began to see who and what Garth really was."

"How did you meet him? Was he from this area?"

Sighing, she shook her head. "No. I met him through a mutual friend, while I was in college down at Phoenix. At that time Garth did have an office job selling supplies to area mining companies. He'd often bragged that he'd soon be moving to an executive position and I believed him. He seemed full of ambition and talked continually about wanting to become a family man and filling a house with kids."

"Obviously something happened to change all that."

"Obviously," she repeated with plenty of sarcasm. "Once we were married he quickly lost all interest in his job, and eventually me. Pretty soon he was coming up with all kinds of excuses for missing work. For making endless trips to Phoenix instead of spending time with his wife. Stupidly, I thought having a baby would turn him around and bring us together. It only made things worse and proved to me and my family that Garth was incapable of being a responsible man."

"I'm sorry, Viv."

"Don't be. I did get one child from the man," she said with wry acceptance. "As for the house, he'd always asked, why make an effort to find us a house, when we have everything we need right here. Bah! He hated living here on the ranch, secluded from the lights of the city and all his friends."

The sadness and shame the man must have put Vivian through was impossible for Sawyer to imagine. But he did know one thing, if he ever happened to accidentally run into the jerk, he'd knock him out cold.

"Do you think he ever loved you?"

She looked at him and even in the semidarkness, he could see her lips were quivering as she tried to smile. The image caused a pain to squeeze the middle of his chest.

"No. It was all a farce. But that fact quit bothering me years ago. What breaks my heart is that because of my foolish judgment, Hannah has been deprived of a real father. She isn't dumb or totally naive, Sawyer. She figured out a long time ago that he cared nothing for her."

And Sawyer had always considered his mother to be a

bad parent, he thought sickly. At least she'd hung around and made an attempt to be a parent until her son was eight years old. That was more than Hannah had ever gotten from her father.

"A rejection like that is something you don't forget, Viv."

"I guess you would know all about that."

Sighing, she slipped from the rock ledge and turned to face the fire. As Sawyer watched her stretch her hands toward the warmth of the flames, he realized he never wanted her to be hurt again. Not by him or any man.

Then you'd better back away, Sawyer. Let her find someone who will really love her and give her the home and family she deserves. You can't do that.

The voice going off in his head left a hollow feeling in the pit of his stomach. How could he back away from Vivian now? She was beginning to loosen up and see him as more than a coworker. Even more than a flirt. Wasn't that what he wanted more than anything?

Trying to shove the worrisome questions aside, he said, "After hearing this about your ex I'm even more surprised that Hannah seems to like me. If I were in her shoes, I probably wouldn't want my mother to see any man. No matter if he was well-meaning."

Her doubtful gaze lifted to meet his. "You make it sound like Hannah views the two of us as…more than friends?"

Just looking at her plush lips caused desire to stir deep within him. "We are more than friends. Aren't we?"

"How can we be? Our work—"

"We're not at work. We're alone. In the dark. By a warm…cozy…fire."

As the last word passed his lips, he reached for her and pulled her toward him until she was standing between his parted legs, her face only inches from his.

"Sawyer, I—"

Her hands flattened against his chest as though she intended to push him away, but after a brief pause, they slid upward to wrap tightly over his shoulders.

"I'm not sure about this. About me. Or you. Or anything."

His hands slipped around her waist and subtly urged her closer. "What's there to be sure about? I want to kiss you. And I believe you want to kiss me just as much."

"Just because I want to doesn't make it…a wise thing to do."

He traced a fingertip over her cheek and down to the tiny cleft in her chin. "Kissing isn't about being wise, Viv. It's supposed to be enjoyable."

The corners of her lips curved impishly upward. "You're so naughty," she murmured.

"And you're so prim. Mix the two and we'll come out just right."

She groaned with misgivings and then Sawyer felt a thrill of triumph as she closed the distance between their faces and placed her lips on his.

The taste of her amazed him. Like the sweetness of ripe fruit, it called to the hunger deep inside him. And the more he drank from her lips, the more he wanted.

Behind them, the blazing mesquite popped and crackled, while inside Sawyer's head everything was melting into delicious oblivion. He wanted her and she wanted him. Beyond that point, he wasn't going to let anything stand between them.

When her mouth opened to invite his tongue inside, he obliged by thrusting it between her teeth and running the tip against the ribbed roof. The loud rush of blood in his ears very nearly drowned out her needy groan, but he heard it and the sound pushed him further into a pool of desire.

At some point she moved closer and wrapped her arms tightly around his neck. The front of her body was crushed against his and through the fabric of her sweater, he could feel her soft breasts molding to his chest and the rapid thump of her heart was knocking at his, as though to tell him she was kissing him with far more than her lips.

Was this how it felt like for a man to yearn for only one woman? To want her fiercely, recklessly, with little thought for tomorrow? If so, then he'd already lost his freedom.

The warning bells clanging in the back of his head couldn't compete with the pleasure of her kiss and he continued to search her lips, to hold her soft, warm body next to his. The notion of ending the embrace never entered his thoughts until the door of the house opened and Hannah's voice called out.

"Mom!"

Like a sudden explosion, the sound ripped them apart. Vivian whirled away from him and stepped toward the sound of Hannah's voice. Sawyer was too stunned to do much more than swipe a hand through his hair and try to catch his breath.

"We're here by the fire," Vivian answered.

Continuing to stand in the doorway, Hannah relayed her message. "Reeva's made hot chocolate and we're going to roast marshmallows."

"Okay, honey. We'll be right there," Vivian told her.

After Hannah stepped back into the house and closed the door behind her, Vivian returned to where Sawyer was still seated by the fire.

With a rueful slant to her lips, she said, "Family calls. Are you ready for another round?"

He was ready, all right. To have her back in his arms. But to his chagrin, that was going to have to wait for a better time and place. He had no idea where that might be, or whether she'd be willing to give him a second round of kisses. But somehow he'd make it happen.

Rising to his feet, he reached for her hand. She squeezed his fingers and a ridiculous thrill rushed through him. Being here with Vivian tonight was changing him. And he wasn't quite sure if the changes were making him a better man or a gullible fool.

"Sure, I'm ready. Uh—unless I have your lipstick on my mouth."

She looked at him. "You don't have a thing on your mouth, except a grin."

And her family, particularly her brothers, might get the wrong idea, he thought. "Should I wipe it off?"

"No. I like your mouth just like it is."

They stepped back into the den with the grin still on his face.

Chapter Ten

The next evening, as the sun rapidly sank behind the desert hills, Vivian stood to one side of the large crowd that had gathered to enjoy the Christmas caroling service. So far the event had gone off without a hitch and everyone seemed to be in high, holiday spirits.

She was singing along to a traditional hymn, while keeping an eye out for any kind of misbehavior in the crowd, when Sawyer walked up and stood just to her left. Since the service had started, she'd hardly gotten to say more than two words to him, but they'd crossed paths earlier and the faint smile he'd given her had settled in her heart like a sweet kiss.

"Mort should be happy with tonight's outcome," Sawyer said. "Everyone seems to be having a great time."

"Not me!" Zane announced as he walked up on the opposite side of Sawyer. "When are those singers going to start rockin'? I want to hear something like 'Santa, Baby.'"

"What they need to sing for you is 'I'm Gettin' Nuttin' for Christmas,'" Sawyer teased his friend.

Vivian laughed and sang, "'Cause he ain't been nuttin' but bad."

"Aww, come on, you two. I'm the kindest, sweetest ranger at this park."

Sawyer shot him a look of disbelief and Zane laughed.

"Okay," he relented. "Vivian probably gets the sweetest vote. But I'm good and kind."

"Well, maybe Santa will surprise us all and make a stop at your house. I wouldn't hold my breath, though," Sawyer advised him.

"Sheesh, and here I was thinking I was getting a new sports car." He slanted Sawyer a sly look. "But I guess last night at the Fandango crossed that off Santa's list for me. By the way, Sawyer, I didn't see you there. You must have been doing your dancing somewhere else."

As best as Vivian could remember, the Fandango was a rowdy dancehall/saloon on the far outskirts of Wickenburg. Her brother Joseph and his fellow deputies were often called to the premises for brawls, along with other types of drunken, unruly behavior.

"I haven't been to the Fandango in ages," Sawyer told him, then exchanged a private glance with Vivian. "And last night I was—doing something else."

Whether Zane picked up on the connection between her and Sawyer, she couldn't say. At least he was Sawyer's friend and Vivian could only hope he wasn't the type of man to spread rumors.

Oh, Lord, how was this all going to end? Last night with Sawyer had been one of the happiest she'd had in more years than she could remember. Having him by her side to share in the Christmas festivities had made everything special. And when he'd kissed her...the thought of it still left her tingling and aching to be back in his arms.

"Yeah, something else," Zane said with a cunning chuckle. "I'm sure that something else was blonde or brunette and about five foot two."

"What do you know?" Sawyer asked, clearly annoyed with his friend. "She might've been a redhead."

"Aw, that's right, you like 'em all."

"Don't you have something else to do?" Sawyer asked sharply.

Zane chuckled, then after a quick glance to his left, he said, "Uh, yeah, I do. There's Mort at the back of the crowd and he's staring right at me."

He walked away and Sawyer cast her a sheepish glance. "Sorry about that, Viv. Zane is—well—"

"Just being himself," she finished stiffly. "You don't have to apologize for your friend. He seems to know you quite well."

Frowning, he moved close enough to speak in her ear. "I was out with you last night, remember? And I haven't had a real girlfriend in ages!"

Vivian couldn't decide whether she wanted to laugh or take off running. "Can you define what a *real* girlfriend means?"

"Well, it means a girl that I dated a few times—on a regular basis."

"Oh. And what do you call the other ones?"

The frown on his face deepened. "I don't have any other ones," he said, then shook his head. "Okay, I confess, I tried to have a date last weekend. It didn't work. And I ended up taking her home before the evening started. Thanks to you."

"Me?" She tried to laugh, but the sound was hardly one

of amusement. "Sorry, Sawyer. I was out of line. Your dating habits are none of my business."

"Viv, are you…angry with me?"

She wasn't angry. She was sick with jealousy and that made her more than stupid.

"Of course not. I have no reason to be angry with you." Glancing away from him, she searched for a reason to make a quick exit and found it when she spotted an unusually long line outside the women's restroom. "Excuse me, Sawyer. Looks like there might be a problem at the restroom."

She walked off, while thinking she'd come very close to making herself look like a jealous fool over a man who didn't belong to her, or any woman.

For next half hour Sawyer wanted to catch up with Zane and choke the life out of him. The man didn't know when to keep his mouth shut.

But by the time the caroling ended and the crowd began to disperse, he'd forgiven his buddy's untimely remarks.

Zane was just being the happy-go-lucky jokester he'd always been. Besides, his friend had no idea that Sawyer was romantically interested in Vivian.

Romantically interested, hell! That couldn't begin to describe the feelings he had for Vivian. But with a woman like her, how far could those feelings take him? Plucking a star from the sky would be easier than gaining Vivian's love.

Love? No. That wasn't what he wanted, Sawyer firmly repeated to himself as he helped move a stack of folding chairs into a storage building. Love didn't last any more than hot sex. Ultimately, it all ended.

"Looks like that's it for tonight." Zane locked the storage building and turned to Sawyer. "Want to go grab a drink at Burro Crossing?"

"No, thanks." He glanced around in hopes of catching a glimpse of Vivian. Ever since she'd walked away from him earlier this evening, he'd not crossed paths with her and he'd gotten the impression that she was purposely keeping her distance. "I think—" He broke off midsentence as he suddenly spotted Vivian walking toward her vehicle. "Excuse me, Zane. I'll see you later."

He hurried across the dimly lit parking lot and managed to reach her side just as she was opening the door on the truck.

"Viv, are you leaving?" he asked.

She turned toward him and from the look on her face, she was surprised to see him.

"In case you haven't noticed, the services are over," she said, "and Mort has dismissed us."

"I know. But—" he moved a step closer and lowered his voice, even though the parking lot was practically empty and no one was in hearing distance "—I thought you'd at least say goodbye before you left."

She smiled up at him, but he could see the expression was strained. "You were busy. And I didn't want to bother you."

Her voice was as stiff as a starched shirt and although she'd said she wasn't angry with him, something was definitely wrong.

"Bother me? Why don't you just come out and say you're trying to give me the brush-off?"

She sighed and he could see her features begin to soften.

"That would hardly be possible, Sawyer. We work together. I'll see you first thing in the morning."

"Working together is not what I'm talking about. Last

night, when I left Three Rivers, you were happy. And that kiss on the patio—I thought you meant it."

"Meant what?" she asked casually, then shook her head. "I'm just like you, Sawyer, I can enjoy a kiss just for the physical pleasure of it. After all, you said kisses were something to be enjoyed."

His grandmother used to warn him that his philandering ways would one day come back to haunt him. He'd always laughed at the idea. After all, how could any of it haunt him when he was more than glad to move from one woman to the next? He should've known his grandmother was never wrong.

"Viv, please—"

She darted a glance at the opposite end of the parking lot where the last of the extra rangers were driving away.

"Look, Sawyer, I've been thinking and it's not hard for me to figure out—this connection between us—isn't going to work."

The flatness of her voice scared him and in that moment, he realized that his world would be a very dark place without her.

He reached for her hand and captured its softness against his chest. "You're wrong about us, Viv. And you have me wrong."

Her gaze dropped to the ground. "You really need to let me go—home."

Home was with him. The thought was crazy but he couldn't push it out of his mind.

"It's still early. I thought we might drive over to Burro Crossing and have coffee."

Disbelief parted her lips. "Now?"

His hand tightened around hers. "Sure, right now. They have great pie, too. Cherry. Pecan. Chocolate meringue."

She studied him for long moments and then to his immense relief, a tiny smile of surrender touched her lips. "Cherry, you say?"

"With ice cream if you'd like."

She groaned. "Okay. Against my better judgment, I'll follow you."

Vivian couldn't remember the last time she'd been to Burro Crossing. Most likely about two years ago when she'd made a trip with Holt up to Flagstaff to purchase several horses to add to Three Rivers' remuda. But she recalled exactly where the old adobe bar and grill was located off the highway.

All through the fifteen-minute drive, she'd been giving herself a lecture about putting some common sense to use. As much as she wanted the man, she'd been right when she'd told him it wouldn't work. He wasn't a one-woman man and at his young age, it might be years before he got the urge to settle down. Or he might decide he never wanted to be tied to a wife and kids.

An affair wasn't her style, she mentally argued. An affair would only lead her straight into a pit of quicksand. Yet here she was driving fifteen extra miles just to spend a few more minutes with the man. When was she going to get a grip? After her heart was lying crushed and broken on the floor?

By the time she pulled into the graveled parking area, Vivian had convinced herself that having coffee and pie with Sawyer wasn't going to bring on a major heartbreak. Whether he had a hundred girls waiting for him up at Camp Verde didn't matter. Spending time with him made her feel good and happy. It wasn't like she was going to make the fatal mistake of falling in love with him.

She parked next to his truck and after pulling on a red fleece jacket, she grabbed her handbag from the back seat.

Sawyer was waiting outside the vehicle to help her to the ground and as they walked to the building, he kept a firm hold on her hand. The sweet connection rattled Vivian and try as she might, she couldn't shake off the odd feeling that her life was about to change.

Inside the dimly lit grill, they took a seat in a corner booth. Other than three grizzled-looking men nursing mugs of beer at the bar, she and Sawyer were the only patrons at this late hour.

They'd barely gotten settled when a tired-looking waitress with a messy blond bun emerged from a door behind the bar. She immediately carried two glasses of ice water, along with a couple of menus, to their table.

After she left to fetch their orders, Vivian said, "With this place being on your way home you probably stop here often."

"It is on my way home, but I don't stop that much. Zane and I eat here occasionally. But most of the time I get on home so I can eat with Grandmother."

His grandmother. Just when Vivian was convinced he was nothing more than a flirt and a womanizer, she was reminded of the devotion he held for the woman who'd raised him from a very small boy, and her heart softened to a pile of mush.

"I'm sure she enjoys your company." *I do*, she could've added, but recognized the words were needless. He could see for himself that she couldn't resist his company.

"She likes having me around," he admitted. "But she isn't a demanding person. And never tries to butt into my life."

"Hmm. You're fortunate. Usually older folks get whiney and demanding," Vivian remarked. "She sounds independent like Sam."

He grinned at the mention of the old Bar X foreman.

"I really enjoyed visiting with Sam last night. He told me a bit about Tessa and the background of how she happened to come to Arizona. I can't imagine how shocked she must've been to learn her father was actually the late Sheriff Ray Maddox."

"Well, I think Joe and Tessa began to suspect the truth before they ever found the proof. I do know that it's all been great for Sam. He was so lost after Ray died. Now Tessa and Joe have made him a part of their family. And the ranch is going strong again."

The waitress arrived with their orders and as they began to eat, he said, "Everybody needs somebody."

She studied him for a long moment. "You have your grandmother. But do you ever want more?"

He looked at her as he lowered his fork back to the plate. "I have a feeling that no matter how I answer that question I'm going to be in trouble with you."

She shook her head. "It's not a trick question, Sawyer. Just be honest with me."

He looked so uncomfortable that Vivian feared he might actually bolt from the building, but then he shrugged and dug back into his pie.

"Okay," he said. "I'll be honest. Are you asking me whether I ever want a wife and kids of my own?"

She'd not intended to steer the conversation in this direction and now that she had, she felt a bit foolish. There were no strings tying the two of them together. She couldn't even call herself his girlfriend. That probably made his feelings about love and marriage none of her business. But after that episode on the patio last night, she felt she had a right to know that much about him.

"I do wonder if you ever hanker for a family," she said. "Or if you even want *one* special lady in your life— instead of a merry-go-round of women."

He scowled. "You've been listening to too many rumors."

"No. I've been listening to you. I can see how you're thinking—"

"No," he interrupted, "you can't see. Sure, I've gone out on plenty of dates. Some of the women I liked more than others. But none of them ever got any false promises from me. I've never pretended with them or with you."

That much was true. He'd not made her any sort of pledges or promises. So what was she expecting from him? Too much, too soon, she decided, while realizing the problem wasn't with Sawyer, it was with her. She wanted far more from him than he was willing or able to give.

Reaching across the table, she touched the tip of her fingers to his. "I'm sorry, Sawyer. I don't know what's gotten into me. I guess I'm a little frightened about—well, whatever this is that's happening between us."

A faint smile curved his lips. "If you want me to be honest, then I have to admit that I'm a little scared myself. But not enough to make me back away."

You're the lonely, independent, I-don't-need-a-man-after-Garth kind.

Her mother's reproving words suddenly drifted through Vivian's mind and she realized that, for many years now, she'd been all those things and more. Lonely, yet determined to keep her heart safely cocooned so that no man could reach it. Deep down, she understood that kind of thinking had caused her to miss out on so much living. Even worse, it was still preventing her from reaching for the things she wanted most.

Her gaze met his and the desire she saw stirring in his eyes caused her heart to thump with anticipation.

"I'm not going to back away, either," she said softly. "Not until you tell me to."

With his gaze firmly locked on hers, he wrapped his hand around her fingers. "That's not going to happen."

An electric storm must be bearing down on them, she decided. The hold he had on her hand was shooting hot tingles straight up her arm, while the air between them was practically crackling with energy.

"You sound awfully certain of that," she murmured.

He inclined his head toward her pie. "Let's eat up so we can get out of here."

Five minutes later, with food still on their plates and coffee cooling in their cups, Sawyer paid for the small meal and they left the bar and grill.

By now the night sky was filled with thousands of stars and a cool wind was blowing from the north. Any other time Vivian would've been shivering from the drop in temperature. But tonight, with Sawyer's arm wrapped around the back of her waist, she felt a fire building inside her.

When they reached the spot where their vehicles were parked side by side, he led her to the small space between the truck cabs, where they'd be shielded from view of any passing motorist or patron leaving the bar and grill.

Vivian wasn't surprised when he pulled her into his arms. Nor did she dream about resisting as his mouth came down on hers. Earlier she'd felt a change coming over her and now as he kissed her, she understood what it meant. Something inside her had finally started letting go. All the doubts, and fears, and questions that had been whirling around in her head were dissolving like raindrops on the desert floor.

When his mouth finally eased from hers, he spoke fervently against her cheek. "I've been wanting to do that all day. Every time I'm near you I want to gather you close in my arms and never let go."

Stunned by the feelings he evoked in her, she reached

up and cradled his face with both hands. "I want the same thing, too," she admitted.

"Oh, Viv. My sweet Viv."

Once again he covered her lips with his, only this time his kiss was desperate and all-consuming. She could think of nothing but the reckless mating of their mouths and the way his hands had found their way beneath her jacket to cup around both breasts.

Streaks of white-hot desire were racing through her, heating her skin and causing her heart to beat at a frantic pace. By the time he lifted his head, she recognized her arms were wrapped tightly around his neck, while the front of her body was crushed against a wall of hard, warm muscles.

"We can't keep standing here like this. I think...we need to...uh, go somewhere quiet and private."

She understood exactly what he was suggesting and the mere thought of being *that* alone with him was enough to cause her voice to drop to a husky rasp. "Yes—I think so, too. But where?"

He pondered her question for only a moment before he said, "I know a place. But it's more than a half hour away. Burro Crossing is open all night so it should be safe to leave your truck here and I'll drive us there."

She didn't stop to second-guess him or herself. She was tired of wondering how it would be to have Sawyer make love to her. Tired of being a woman in hiding.

"All right," she told him. "On the way I'll text my mother and let her know I'm having a late dinner with you before I head home."

He feigned a shocked gasp. "Won't that be telling her a fib?"

"Not entirely. We did have a few bites of pie."

He clicked his tongue in shameful fashion. "Naughty girl. I must be rubbing off on you."

* * *

Forty long minutes later they reached the Camp Verde Indian reservation. Sawyer took a narrow dirt road that led through red rock bluffs and low hills sparsely dotted with tall trees. Eventually, he stopped the truck in front of a small wood-framed house partially hidden behind a cluster of mesquite trees.

"Is this your place?" she asked, as he helped her to the ground.

"Yes. My late uncle Willy left it to me years ago when I was still a teenager. I was the only immediate family he had." He reached for her hand. "Better hang on to me until we reach the door. The ground is rough and there's no yard light."

"Do you have electricity here?" she asked.

"Yes. I keep it and the water on. Since my grandmother's home is a few miles on the other side of the reservation, I rarely get by this way. But I like to have the utilities. Makes it easier to keep the place clean," he explained.

They stepped onto the planked floor of a deep porch, and Sawyer fished a key from his jeans pocket and unlocked the door. After he reached inside and flipped on the light, he ushered her inside the house.

"This is cozy," she commented as she gazed curiously around the small room.

Watching her reaction, Sawyer tried to imagine what it looked like through her eyes. The furniture dated back to the midseventies and the flowered wallpaper had faded from the heat and sunlight. Brown patterned linoleum was worn through in spots to expose the wood subflooring, but it was clean, as was the rest of the house.

He walked over to a small gas heater and turned the thermostat to high. "Not anything like Three Rivers," he replied. "But I've always been proud to call it mine. One of these years I might decide to fix it up. But I kinda like it like this because it reminds me of my uncle. And my dad. The two brothers were close and Dad always brought me with him when he came here to visit."

"I wouldn't do a thing to it." She stepped to the middle of the room. "And let me tell you, this house is grand compared to the little cabin my great-great-grandparents lived in. It's the original ranch house. And other than making repairs to keep it intact, we haven't altered it."

"Sounds interesting."

"It is. One of these days I'll show it to you."

"I like the sound of that." He came up behind her and slipped his arms around her waist, then bending his head, he nuzzled his nose against the side of her neck. "I'm sorry about the long drive to get here. I hope it didn't give you too much time to think."

She twisted around until she was facing him. "You mean about being here with you?"

She felt warm and oh, so soft in his arms. He didn't think he could ever get tired of touching her, hearing her voice or resting his eyes on her lovely face.

"Something like that," he murmured.

Tilting her head back, she gave him a provocative smile that lit her eyes with all sorts of promises. "If you're wondering if I'm having second thoughts, I'm not."

The thrill that rushed through him was so strong and unexpected that for a moment he wondered if his boots were actually touching the floor.

"Then you won't mind if I wait to show you the rest of the house?" he asked huskily.

"I won't mind at all."

Groaning with need, he lowered his lips to hers. The contact created an instant combustion and after a few short moments they were wrapped in each other's arms, their mouths fused together.

Raw desire shot through him and sparked a fire deep in his loins.

Sawyer couldn't remember ever wanting a woman the way he wanted Vivian. Nor could he begin to understand the tangled feelings swirling through him. Was this his body crying out for sexual release? Or his heart pining to love her? Really love her?

Tonight he couldn't allow himself think about the what, or the why. In fact, he didn't want to think at all. He only wanted to feel the exquisite pleasure of having her body next to his. And with that sole intention, he eased his mouth from hers and lifted her into his arms.

With her arms latched tightly around his neck, he carried her down a short hallway and entered a door to their right. The room was subtly lit with shafts of moonlight slanting through a bare window. The illumination was enough for him to see his way to the bed and once he reached the side of it, he set her back on her feet.

"There's a clean quilt on the bed, but no sheets," he told her. "I don't bother with those because no one ever sleeps here."

"No one?"

His hands cradled her face as he brought the tip of his nose to hers. "In case that wicked little mind of yours is working overtime, you happen to be the first and only woman I've ever brought here. Can you believe me?"

"I don't think you'd lie about that. But I am wondering why me? And why this place?"

He rubbed his lips over her cheek, then down toward the corner of her mouth. "Because you're the only woman I would ever want to share this place with. It's special. Like you."

"Sawyer, please—you don't have to shower me with sweet words just to make me feel like I'm not—"

"About to leap off a tall, rocky cliff," he finished wryly.

She lifted her gaze up to his face, and the desire he saw in her green eyes not only humbled him, it left him feeling ashamed and afraid.

"It's a mighty tall leap for me," she whispered.

Groaning, he thrust his hands into her hair and cradled the back of her head. "I've been a fool, Viv. And I'm sorry. More sorry than I've ever been about anything."

A line furrowed the smooth skin between her brows. "Sawyer, what are you apologizing for? Pursuing me?"

"No. I'm not sorry about that. I'm thanking God that I had enough guts to pursue a woman like you. But I—well, I want you to know that the first day we met—I took one look at you and decided I had to have sex with you. And that was all I wanted."

Her nostrils flared and he figured he'd just blown this night and probably any chance at another. Yet he didn't regret his confession. She deserved that much from him.

"In other words you wanted to seduce me and to hell with my feelings? Right?"

He cringed. Somehow hearing her speak his plans out loud made them sound ten times worse. "That's a mighty caustic way of putting it. But—you are right. That first day I saw you as a conquest. By the next day everything changed. You'd already become my friend and partner. You'd become special to me."

Doubt flickered across her face. "That quick?"

His thumbs gently smoothed across her cheekbones. "That quick. And now—I don't know what any of this means, Viv. I only know that something is growing between us and I don't want to ignore it. I want us to be together—to give each other pleasure—to be happy."

"Happy, yes. That's what I want, too," she whispered. "But what about our work? You're only going to be at Lake Pleasant for a few months. Still, this intimate connection between us could jeopardize our jobs—our careers. I don't want that, Sawyer."

"We won't let that happen, Viv. On the job we'll simply be rangers working together. That's all anyone will ever see," he said with gentle assurance.

"Yes. Just two rangers doing our job," she agreed, then rising on the tips of her toes, she placed her lips against his.

"Mmm. Does this mean you don't want to leave?"

"It means you've done enough talking for now."

She was right. The time had come for him to show her exactly how much he wanted her. But was he ready for her to see the tender feelings that were budding in his heart?

No. He wasn't brave enough to be that vulnerable. He wasn't sure he'd ever be.

Chapter Eleven

Vivian wasn't sure how it happened so quickly. One minute they'd been kissing and the next he was tossing her clothing into a nearby chair and easing her back onto the double bed.

The quilt was cool to her bare back and the mattress was lumpy, but her senses barely registered those things as she watched Sawyer strip down to a pair of dark-colored boxers. His long, lean body was everything she'd thought it would be and more. Much more, she realized, as her gaze drifted downward to the erection pushing against the fabric of his underwear.

Did he already want her that much? Was he expecting her to be experienced? The notion that she might not be able to please him, especially since she'd not made love to a man since her divorce, made her so anxious she began to tremble.

He joined her on the bed and the moment he pulled her

into his arms he felt the tremors that had taken control of her body.

"Viv, what's wrong? Are you cold?"

"No. I—" She buried her face in his shoulder and clung to him tightly. "I'm worried this is not going to go well for you. I'm— It's been so long—I think I've forgotten how to make love."

He eased her head back far enough to look at her face and the tenderness she spotted in his eyes was so sweet, so unexpected, that tears suddenly burned her throat.

"Oh, my precious Viv. Don't worry. Don't think about anything. Except the two of us. And this."

His lips came softly down on hers and in that moment she realized that Sawyer was going to be a giving and patient lover. And that was more than enough to give her the confidence she'd lost all those years ago when her marriage had collapsed.

After pressing a series of light kisses on her lips and cheeks, he lifted his head and with one hand, speared fingers into her hair.

As he spread the chestnut tresses over the quilt, he murmured, "The moonlight has turned your hair into flames dipped in silver. And my kisses have changed the color of your lips to a shade of crushed cherries." To emphasize his words, his forefinger softly outlined the shape of her lips until they quivered beneath his touch. "You don't look like a ranger now. You look like a very sexy woman—my woman."

"Oh, yes, Sawyer. Make me your woman—in every way."

The whispered plea was all he needed to hear and as he dropped his mouth to one puckered nipple, she was sure the floor tilted and the tiny room morphed into a patch of paradise.

Over and over, he laved her breasts with his lips and tongue, while his hands roamed over the hills and valleys of her curves, the long length of her muscled legs. Each time she thought she couldn't feel more, she did, until finally the sensations were so many and flying at her with such speed that her throbbing body began to ache for relief.

She was writhing beneath him, her hands racing over the heated skin of his back and shoulders, when his fingers slipped between her thighs and urged them apart.

A gasp of pleasure rushed past her lips as his fingers touched the most intimate part of her, and when she dared to lift her eyes to his face, she saw that he was smiling down at her. And she realized he was taking immense pleasure in giving to her, instead of quickly taking what she was offering.

"You're so lovely, Viv. So perfect—for me."

She tried to form a reply, but she was too overcome with emotions to utter a word. And then speaking was no longer important as his fingers began to stroke the wet folds that were aching to receive him.

Intense pleasure washed over her in undulating waves and she cried out as she clung to his arms in an effort to prevent herself from being totally swept away. Then, just as she was teetering on the brink of losing all grip on her senses, he suddenly eased away from her and stood at the side of the bed.

The abrupt separation confused her. Until she saw him pulling a small packet from his wallet.

"I'm glad you came prepared," she said awkwardly. "I haven't taken birth control in years."

"I wasn't sure when or if this would ever happen. But I wanted to be ready."

He turned his back to deal with the protection, then returned to the bed. She reached eagerly for him and with a needy groan he positioned himself over her.

"I never thought I'd ever want a man like this," she told him. "Not ever again. But somehow you've changed me, Sawyer. And now all I want is you—inside of me—loving me."

"Viv."

The shortened version of her name was all he said before he lowered his hips and entered her with one slow, delicious thrust.

This wasn't supposed to happen like this, Sawyer thought. He hadn't planned on feeling this way. Not tonight. Not ever. But the wild, reckless need that gripped his senses was far too strong to fight. Vivian and her warm, giving body had taken total control of him and he was like a fallen leaf, tumbling helplessly end over end, with only a wayward wind to guide it.

Loving me. Loving me. Her words were like a mantra in his brain and with each thrust of his body, he tried to shove them away, tried to convince himself that every glorious burst of pleasure racking his body had nothing to do with his heart.

But then he would take one look at her sweet face and his lips would return to hers and he'd close his eyes against the onslaught of emotions. And the whole reckless circle would start all over again.

When he finally felt himself climbing toward the finish, he felt a sense of triumph that he'd survived the storm. Yet when the end finally came and he felt Vivian arching desperately toward him, felt her arms and legs banding tightly around him, he wasn't prepared for the utter surrender of his mind and his body. Everything inside him was pouring into her and he knew with certain finality that he'd never get it back.

Long moments passed before he found the strength to roll away from her, and even then his breathing was little more than short, ragged gulps. Next to him, Vivian remained on her back with her eyes closed, her swollen lips slightly parted. Except for the rapid rise and fall of her chest, she was motionless and Sawyer wondered what she was thinking, feeling. He couldn't imagine it being anything close to the upheaval going on inside of him.

After a moment, she rolled toward him and curled her body into his. "I wish we had a blanket to cover up with," she murmured drowsily. "But then I'd get too comfortable."

"What would be wrong with that?" he asked, while being grateful he was still able to speak.

"It's getting late. And I'm well over an hour's drive from home."

"Will anyone in your family be waiting up to make sure you make it home okay? Your mother maybe?"

"I've had to work late before. Sometimes overnight. All my family will go to bed and check with me in the morning. What about your grandmother?"

"I warned her I'd be late. She doesn't worry."

Sighing, she nestled her cheek against the hollow of his shoulder. "Well, maybe we could stay just a few minutes longer," she said wistfully.

"If that's the way you feel, then don't move. I'll be right back."

He left the bed and crossed the floor to an old chest of drawers. After he pulled a folded quilt from the bottom drawer, he returned to the bed and draped the cover over her. "Your wish is my command. This should make you cozy."

"I'll be cozier with you next to me," she said.

He joined her beneath the quilt and as he gathered her close against him, he tried to imagine having endless nights with her by his side. How would it be to always have her sleeping next to him? To know their days and nights and hopes and dreams would all be shared together?

"This is nice."

"Mmm. Much better than pie and coffee." She slid her palm across his chest and down his abdomen. "Although some toast and scrambled eggs would be wonderful right now."

He chuckled. "Sorry. The fridge is empty."

"It's very quiet here," she commented. "Are there any neighbors around? When we drove up I didn't notice any houses nearby."

"There are two homes just over the hill from here. Both of those families keep an eye out on the place for me. Fortunately I've never had any vandal problems."

"Did your uncle always live here alone?"

"He was a rodeo cowboy and was gone for most of the time following the circuit. A wife or kids wouldn't have fit his lifestyle. I think he had a special woman at one time in his life, but she died at a very young age. After that I don't think he ever wanted another one."

"That's very sad. It sounds like your father and your uncle both suffered in the love department."

That was something that Sawyer tried not to think about. Especially since he'd met Vivian. He didn't want to think all the Whitehorse men were cursed when it came to women.

He rubbed a hand over his face then dropped his fingers to her hair. As he twined them through the silky strands, he said, "I often wonder if my father was ever loved. It didn't seem so. But then I saw my parents' relationship through a child's eye. My grandmother said that Onida was never a good wife or mother. And I guess that much is obvious with her leaving and never coming back. Still, there are moments when I think she must have loved my father at one time—in the beginning. Why else would she have married him and bore him a child? I wonder, too, if he didn't know how to make her happy or be a husband to her. I guess I'll never know."

"Not unless your mother returns someday."

He tilted his head so that he could look down at her. "I told you that we'd heard from an old acquaintance that Onida died."

"I wouldn't put much stock in that rumor. Just like my family doesn't believe my father's death was an accident. One thing for sure. There's no chance of Dad ever coming back. But there's still a possibility you might see your mother someday. How would you feel about that?"

Over the years Sawyer had carried a load of anger and resentment over the woman who'd given birth to him. In fact, his heart had so hardened toward her, he'd refused to label her as his mother. Yet now that Vivian had come into his life, he was looking at everything through different eyes. He was beginning to wonder if Onida had left Arizona for reasons other than to rid herself of the responsibilities of a son.

"I honestly don't know, Viv. There are some things I'd like to have answered."

She sighed and her warm breath caressed his skin. The sensation stirred his senses. Just like the touch of her hand skimming along his rib cage and the womanly scent of her skin rising up to his nostrils.

"Answers," she said quietly. "Most people go through life searching for those."

He bent his head in order to press a kiss on her temple. "Well, you've answered a very important question tonight."

She lifted her head to look at him. "I have?"

He smiled at her bemused expression. "Yes, you have. You just proved that you haven't forgotten how to make love."

Chuckling under her breath, she brought her lips next to his. "For further proof, here's an early Christmas gift."

After getting only three hours of sleep, Vivian should have felt depleted the next morning. Instead, she felt like she could easily jog two miles and the smile on her face was noticed at the breakfast table by more than one family member.

"The caroling service must have been a humdinger," Holt said as he wolfed down a mountain of scrambled eggs wrapped in a flour tortilla. "You're still singing carols this morning."

She grinned at him. "That's because I'm in the Christmas mood. The holiday is coming fast, little brother. Have you gotten my gift yet?"

"Oh, heck, do I have to buy you a gift this year? A woman who has everything?"

She pulled a face at him. "I rarely go shopping for anything. I don't have time."

"She did have time for dinner with Sawyer last night, though," Maureen spoke up. "And I'm a happy mother for that."

Hoping there wasn't a blush on her face, Vivian looked down the table to where her mother sat at an angle to her father's empty chair.

"Do you really mean that, Mom?"

"I really mean it."

Across the table, Blake said, "It makes us all happy, Viv. We all like your new man."

"Yeah," Holt added, "we just hope you hold on to him."

"Now wait a minute, you two," Vivian practically stuttered. "Sawyer isn't *my* man. I mean—yes, we're more than coworkers. But—"

"You guys are making your sister blush," Katherine said. "You need to lighten up on her."

Grateful to her sister-in-law, Vivian said, "Thanks, Kat. How's the morning sickness?"

Smiling wanly, Katherine pointed to her plate of crackers and fresh fruit. "Better. At least I'm getting something down."

"Good," Vivian said. "Little Katherine needs her nourishment."

"Little Katherine!" Holt shook his head. "You have it wrong, sis. I can tell you right now the baby is definitely a boy."

Vivian rolled her eyes at him. "Since when did you become an authority on pregnancies?"

"I have about thirty pregnant mares right now. And I can correctly predict the gender of eighty-five percent of them before they're born. Just ask Chandler. He knows I'm an expert on the subject."

"Chandler has already left for the clinic this morning," Maureen said. "But we'll all be sure and ask him about your expertise tonight, Holt."

"Actually, Kat could be having a girl and a boy," Blake said coyly.

Everyone around the table stared at him in stunned disbelief, including Vivian. Ever since she'd made love to Sawyer last night, she'd been fantasizing about how it would be to have his child. Yet deep down she knew that's all it could be, an incredible dream. Katherine and Blake were blessed. Their hopes and wishes were actually coming true.

Maureen put down her coffee cup. "Twins! You two

haven't mentioned this possibility before. Are you serious?"

"He is," Katherine answered with another wan smile. "I had a checkup with my OB yesterday. He suspects twins but he can't be sure until I have an ultrasound. That's scheduled for this afternoon."

Holt grinned. "Hell, brother, you're going to get two babies for the price of one!"

"Holt, don't start jumping the gun just yet," Blake warned him. "We don't know for sure."

The likelihood of having twins in the family continued to be tossed around the table as Vivian hurriedly downed the last of her breakfast. By the time she'd left the dining room, Holt had already named his twin nephews and bought them a pair of matching paint ponies.

In the kitchen, Vivian walked over to the cabinet where Reeva, a thin, older woman with a silver-gray ponytail, was chopping cilantro.

"Blake just told us that Kat might be having twins," she said to the cook. "Did you know?"

"Kat mentioned it to me this morning when I remarked on her peaked face. It would be a blessed event having two babies at once, but I'm worried about her health. She can barely eat."

"Don't worry, Reeva. Blake will take good care of her. And she has a fine doctor who'll monitor her closely." She glanced up and down the cabinet counter. "Is my lunch ready to go? I need to get a move on or I'm going to be late for work."

Reeva gestured over her shoulder to the green, insulated lunch box and tall, stainless steel thermos she'd placed on a serving cart. "All ready. I put in extra cookies today. You look like you need them."

Cookies were the last thing she needed, but she'd give

them to Sawyer. Since they'd started working together, she'd learned he could eat two whole lunches at once and never gain an ounce. "Thanks. And quit worrying. You'll get gray hairs that way."

"Hmmp," she snorted. "In case you haven't noticed my hair is already gray. And worrying over this family is my job. Especially when it comes to Maureen."

The mention of her mother caused Vivian to pause. "Mom? What's there to worry about with her? She hasn't been ill."

Reeva put down her chopping knife and leveled a stern look at her. "There's something not right with your mother. She won't tell me what it is, but something is darn sure eating at her. I can see it on her face when she thinks no one is looking. And I can see she's hiding it from you kids."

Vivian could usually spot when something was off with her mother. But if Maureen was purposely trying to hide her worries, that was another matter.

"I hope you're wrong, Reeva. Mom works so hard and she has a lot on her mind. Could be she's like you, concerned about Katherine's health."

Reeva shook her head. "No, this started months ago. After she started digging through those old ranch records and found one of your dad's notebooks."

Vivian recalled her brothers discussing the content of the notebook. The gist of it being that Joel had scheduled a meeting with a cattle buyer in Phoenix on the day following his death; however, no one in the family had recognized the name. Joe had used his resources at the sheriff's department to search for the man's identity, but nothing had showed up. Which most likely meant the name had been an alias. Maureen hadn't seemed upset about the development. Instead, Vivian had gotten the impression she was hopeful.

"I'll talk with her when I get a chance," Vivian assured the cook.

Reeva threw up her hands. "Don't you dare mention anything about the notebook! She'll clam right up!"

"All right, I'll be very subtle. Right now I have to run!"

Grabbing up the thermos and lunch box, she hurried out the kitchen door and in the process very nearly crashed head-on into Hannah.

"Oh, Mom, thank goodness I caught you before you left for work!"

She latched a steadying hold on her daughter's arm, while noticing the girl still had to change her clothes and brush her hair before she left for the school bus stop. "What it is, honey? I'm running behind this morning and it looks like you are, too."

"Will you take me and Nick Christmas shopping to-night? Aunt Kat doesn't feel like going and Uncle Blake is too busy. We need to buy gifts for our teachers and a few of our best friends and we need them before school lets out on Friday. Nothing expensive, I promise."

"Tonight? We'd hardly have time to go to Phoenix or Prescott and get back home at a decent hour," Vivian reasoned.

"I know, Mom, but time is running out! We're okay with just going to Wickenburg. That won't take too long. Please, please!"

Vivian did need to do some shopping herself, but on the other hand, Sawyer had already suggested that the two of them get together after work. Given everything that had happened between them last night, she was anxious to be alone with him again. Yet she didn't want to disappoint her daughter. Especially here at Christmastime.

Perhaps she could invite Sawyer to go shopping with them, she thought. If he found an excuse to turn her down, it would be a fairly good indication of whether he wanted her for more than a bed partner.

With the decision quickly made, she said, "Okay, Hannah. You and Nick be ready. We'll leave as soon as I get home from work."

"What about dinner?"

"We'll go to the Lazy Iguana. How about that?"

Her eyes wide with excitement, she hopped up and down. "Oh, that'd be super, Mom! Thank you! Thank you!"

She kissed Vivian's cheek then raced away. A minute later she could hear her daughter calling up the stairs to her cousin Nick.

Smiling to herself, Vivian hurriedly snatched her jacket from the coat closet and headed out of the house.

Sawyer had never been on a shopping excursion, Christmas or otherwise, with a woman and a pair of kids. And he'd been fairly certain he'd feel like a fish out of water tagging along with the three of them. But when Vivian had explained the reason for the outing and invited him to go along, he'd not hesitated to accept. Mostly because he wanted to be with her, no matter the circumstances.

Now, two hours into the trip and five stores later, he decided that Christmas shopping was much more fun than he'd expected. Especially with Hannah and Nick's comical banter.

"This is the last stop and then we'll eat and head home," Vivian announced to the children as they entered a Western wear store. "So you two be sure and get whatever you need on your shopping list."

"It won't take me long, Aunt Vivian," Nick said. "I know exactly what I'm looking for and I don't want Hannah to see it."

Hannah playfully poked her tongue out at him. "That's

okay, snooty, I don't want you to see what I'm buying in here, either."

Smiling smugly, Nick hurried away and Hannah reached for Sawyer's hand. "Will you come help me, Sawyer?"

He darted a questioning glance at Vivian, who smiled and waved him away. "Don't mind me. I'll go browse around while you two do your shopping."

She walked away and Hannah tugged on his hand. "Over here at the jewelry, Sawyer. Let's hurry before Mom comes back and sees us."

He allowed the girl to lead him over to the opposite side of the store where Western-style jewelry was displayed behind a tall glass counter. A few feet away a saleslady was busy helping an elderly gentleman.

"I'll be with you folks in a few minutes," she promised.

"No hurry," Sawyer told her. "We're just looking."

Hannah tugged on his hand to garner his attention. "I want to pick out something special for Mom. Like some earrings. What do you think?"

He'd never bought earrings for a woman. He'd always purposely avoided buying any type of jewelry for the women who'd come and gone in his life. They always seemed to equate sparkly trinkets with serious intentions and he'd never wanted to give that impression.

"You're asking the wrong guy, Hannah. I don't know much about jewelry."

"But you know a lot about Mom and what she likes."

Did he? There had been times Sawyer had thought he could read everything that was going through Vivian's mind. But after last night at his uncle's old house, he realized there were so many facets to the woman, it would take him years to learn them all.

Was that what he wanted? To spend years with Vivian? *Don't be stupid, Sawyer. You could never keep a woman*

*like her by your side. You might know about sex, but you
don't know a flip about love. How could you? Nobody has
ever loved you, except for your grandmother. And she
doesn't count. She loves you because she's old and soft
and doesn't have anybody else.*

Hating the bitter voice in his head, Sawyer did his best
to shake it away and focus on Hannah.

He said, "I do know that she always wears little dangly
earrings. Mostly with silver and turquoise."

Hannah nodded while gazing at the rows of jewelry beneath the glass. "She has lots of those. I'm thinking coral
would look pretty with her red hair."

"It would look beautiful," he agreed, while thinking
Vivian's hair was the mesmerizing color of a red-gold
sunset. Even when it was mussed it made a glorious halo
around her head.

She looked up and gave him a broad smile. "Uncle Holt
is always telling me that I'll never be as pretty as Mom. But
that's his way of teasing me. He says the inside of Mom is
what makes her so beautiful. I think he's right, don't you?"

Something in the middle of Sawyer's chest twisted into
a tight knot. Hannah was so precious. She deserved a real
father. One who would know exactly how to treat a daughter, to love and support her through bad times and good.
She didn't need a misfit like him, who could only pretend
to be a father.

"Your uncle Holt is very right. So we'd better make
sure we pick out something special for her. I like those,"
he said, pointing to a pair of silver doves set against a
round coral stone.

She took one look at them and let out a little squeal of
delight. The sound was infectious and as she oohed and
aahed, Sawyer found himself chuckling.

"Those are beautiful," Hannah agreed. "And she really likes birds."

"They're doves," Sawyer explained. "They're a symbol of love and peace."

"Then those are perfect! You go find Mom and make sure she doesn't come over this way while I pay and get them wrapped," she told Sawyer.

He gave her a conspiring wink. "Don't worry. I'll keep her busy."

Much later, after they'd returned to Three Rivers and helped the children carry in their packages, Vivian and Sawyer escaped outside for a bit of privacy.

As the two of them strolled slowly toward the mares' paddock, Vivian held on to his strong arm. "I'm keeping you out late again. And I should apologize for that. But I won't. I'm so glad that you're here."

He gave her a faint smile. "I'm glad I'm here, too."

"Thank you for being so patient with the kids. I could tell they really enjoyed your company." She slanted a sly look at him. "You said you didn't know anything about Christmas shopping, but I'm doubting that. You were too good at helping Hannah and Nick pick out just the right gifts."

He chuckled. "It's easy when you're spending someone else's money."

"So are there people you'll be buying for?" she asked curiously. "Your grandmother?"

"I have to be very careful with her. She won't accept anything expensive because she doesn't have the money to buy me a gift of equal value. I'll keep it simple."

By now they had reached the tall board fence that separated the large pasture from the ranch yard. At this time of the year, it was occupied with mares that were due to foal in early January. Several of them trotted over to say hello and search for a treat. Vivian pulled a few peppermints from the pocket on her jacket and gave each one a candy.

"I'd very much like to meet your grandmother," she told him. "Do you think she'd mind?"

There was a long pause before he finally said, "I think she'd like that. But I'm...not sure about you...coming to the reservation."

Resting her back against the fence, she gazed up at him. The security light for this section of the pasture was just enough illumination for her to catch the awkward expression on his face.

Completely puzzled by his reaction, she asked, "What does that mean? I was on the reservation with you last night. Am I not welcome at your home?"

He grimaced. "Of course you're welcome. It's just that—oh, hell, Viv. I might as well just say this plainly."

"I wish you would."

"Okay, once you see how I live, you might have a totally different view of me. You might decide that—uh, the two of us just can't work. Not in the way you're thinking."

She wasn't sure what he meant by that remark and she decided tonight was hardly the time to question him about it.

"Sawyer, that sort of attitude is insulting. Please don't hold it against me because my family is wealthy. Whatever you're thinking, I'm not a snob."

"I never imagined you were. But your family wants the best for you. And I'm not the best. I'm far from it."

Pushing away from the fence, she slipped her arms around his waist and drew her body close to the hard warmth of his. "I think I'm the one who should be deciding that. Don't you?"

A wry smile twisted his lips. "Right now, I think you're irresistible."

Her heart began to thump with eager anticipation. "Then why are you resisting?" she whispered.

His head bent down to hers. "I'm not."

Vivian closed her eyes and then his lips were on hers, searching, coaxing, reminding her of how it felt for their bodies to be completely connected. The kiss went on and on, rocking her senses and sending waves of heat crashing through every inch of her body.

Once it finally ended, she was breathless and her hands were clenched to the front of his shirt.

"You know what I'm thinking?" he asked.

Drawing in a shaky breath, she tilted her head back to look at him. "No. Tell me."

"I'm thinking this Christmas is going to be very special."

As long as she had him in her arms, it would be the most wonderful Christmas of all, she thought.

"Very special indeed," she whispered, then tugged his head back down to hers.

Chapter Twelve

As Christmas Eve rapidly approached, the camping sites in the park filled to capacity. Even the primitive areas that didn't offer electricity or other utilities were jammed with tents and travel trailers. The extra guests created more work for all the rangers at Lake Pleasant, but Vivian hardly noticed. A holiday spirit was putting everyone in a generous mood, making her job easier. Besides, she was too busy wondering where this newfound relationship with Sawyer was going to take her to be dwelling on the heavy workload.

Last evening she and Sawyer had managed to make another trip to his uncle's house and though she'd not thought it possible, the few hours she'd spent in his arms had been even more incredible. Afterward, she'd hoped he would open up and talk to her about the future and his feelings for her. She wanted to believe that somewhere deep in his heart, he was beginning to love her. But he'd not said anything remotely close to the *L* word. Rather he was often pointing out the stark differences between them.

She glanced at him as he made a U-turn in the middle of the road and headed the SUV back in the direction of headquarters. Their work shift was about to end and the thought of not seeing him tonight elicited a sigh from deep within her.

"Are you tired?"

She cast him a faint smile. She hadn't realized he'd heard the despondent sound. Now she needed to make sure he couldn't read her mind. He was like one of the wild colts that Holt trained to the saddle. Making any kind of move that was too fast or abrupt was a surefire way to ruin the chance for a peaceful union.

"I'm not tired. I was just thinking. About how nice it would be to go back to the reservation tonight." She could feel her cheeks growing pink and she wondered if she was becoming the most foolish woman in Yavapai County. After all the heartache and humiliation she'd been through with Garth, she should've known better than to fall in love with a man who considered marriage worse than a case of chicken pox or some other kind of annoying ailment.

"It would be nice," he agreed. "But I've been away from Grandmother far too much here lately."

Nodding, she swallowed back another wistful sigh. "I understand. I've been away from Hannah and my family too much. And I have lots of gift wrapping I need to do tonight. Tomorrow is Christmas Eve. You haven't forgotten, have you?"

He chuckled. "How could I? Every campsite we stop at folks are offering us candy and cookies and wishing us a merry Christmas. Much more of this and we'll both be looking like a pair of fat town dogs."

"Speak for yourself," she teased. "It's a wonderful time

of the year. It reminds me that there's still hope and love
in the world."

He didn't say anything to that and she glanced over to
see his gaze was thoughtfully fixed on the road ahead.

She rubbed a hand up and down her thigh in a nervous
gesture, then berated herself for the silly reaction. This
was Sawyer, the man she'd made love to more than once.
She should be able to ask him most anything.

"Uh, you haven't mentioned your plans, but I was hoping you'd come to Three Rivers and celebrate Christmas
Eve with me and my family tomorrow night. Reeva will
have all sorts of goodies to eat and Holt will play Santa
Claus."

He glanced at her. "You and your family open your gifts
on Christmas Eve?"

"Some of the gifts. The things that Santa brings will be
opened on Christmas Day."

"I see." He cast her a rueful glance. "It sounds like fun,
but I can't make it. I should've already explained to you
that I always spend Christmas Eve with Grandmother. I
don't want to disappoint her."

To say Vivian felt let down would be an understatement,
but she did her best to hide it behind a bright smile. Besides, she truly did understand his situation and admired
him for being so loyal to his grandmother. With her advancing years, he certainly didn't want to miss such a special time with her.

"I understand, Sawyer, and I'm okay with it. As long as
you know you're wanted by me—and my family."

"Thanks for the invitation, Viv."

He glanced at her again and this time Vivian thought
the expression on his face was a bit sheepish, although she
couldn't imagine why.

"Mort asked me if I wanted to work Christmas Day. I

told him if he couldn't find anyone else, I would, but Zane spoke up and offered to work in my place. Did Mort ask you to work that day?"

"No. I think he purposely tries to skip over the rangers who have families, so that they can stay home and celebrate." She started to ask him if he had plans for that day, but as an idea began to form in her mind, she quickly decided not to mention Christmas Day at all.

The next night, after Sawyer and his grandmother finished their meal of fried venison, beans and corn bread, they retired to the living room, where the television was tuned to an oldie station that was broadcasting holiday programs from years past.

In one corner, opposite of the television set, stood a small pine tree that Nashota had chosen from the woods at the back of their property. Before Sawyer had chopped it down, he'd attempted to tell his grandmother that the tree was scraggly with very few limbs to decorate. Yet she'd refused to look for another tree. Instead, she'd talked to him about humility and how the Savior had been born in a stable.

Now as he thought about Nashota's wish to always remain humble and never display a need for things that were out of her reach, he wondered if it was wrong of him to need Vivian so badly. Was it hopeless for him to love her the way his heart ached to love her?

Oh, yes, he'd fallen very, very hard for her. He could admit that much. But admitting his feelings didn't fix anything. Especially when he could see she was growing closer and closer to him. That was something he hadn't wanted or expected. He wanted to simply enjoy being with her while he was at Lake Pleasant and then move on. But now the thought of giving her up to some other man was tearing at him.

What the hell do you want, Sawyer? Vivian is the most precious thing you'll ever have in your life. What are you going to do? Ruin it all by running scared? By letting your parents' disastrous marriage ruin your chance at happiness?

"You're awfully quiet tonight, Sawyer."

He looked over to where Nashota was sitting in the same wooden rocker she'd had for years. Most generally at this time of the evening she would be dragging out her beadwork, but tonight she was simply rocking gently back and forth, her hands lying idly in her lap. Each time Sawyer looked at her gnarled fingers, he thought of how it had been her hands who'd soothed him when, as a child, he'd been frightened or sick. Her hands who'd patted him with encouragement and helped him up after he'd fallen.

"I'm thinking about all you've done for me after my mot—after Onida left," he finished, surprising himself that he'd almost said mother. What was coming over him, anyway? Were his feelings for Vivian making him soft and vulnerable?

Her smile was thoughtful. "And I think about all you've done for me, so we're even, my grandson." She gestured to the sparsely decorated tree. "I have a gift for you. Don't you want to open it?"

As a robed choir on the TV screen sang "Joy to the World," Sawyer collected the wrapped gift he'd purchased for her and the smaller one she had for him.

After placing her gift at her feet, he carried his over to the couch and sat down to open it.

Wrapped inside the green foil paper, he discovered a leather sheath for his knife. Beautifully hand tooled in a feather and sunburst design, the case was fashioned with a clip on the back to attach to his belt. The time and intricate workmanship that his grandmother had put into the gift brought a lump of emotion to his throat.

He looked at her with surprise. "You made this. When? I've not seen you working on it."

She chuckled. "You don't know everything I do around here."

"I guess not. This is beautiful, Grandmother. Thank you." He left the couch and after placing a grateful kiss on her wrinkled cheek, he squatted on his heels next to her rocker.

"Now you open your gift," he urged.

"When did you get this?" she asked. "When you went shopping with Vivian?"

"No. I found it in Camp Verde yesterday. See, you're lucky you even got a gift," he teased.

She reached over and patted his hand that was resting on the arm of her rocker. "You're the only gift I need."

After tearing away the paper, she opened the cardboard to pull out a snow globe perched on a gold filigree base.

Holding it carefully in both palms, Nashota gazed at the wintery scene as though she'd been transported to a dreamland.

"I know how much you'd like to see it snow, but it never does, so now you can shake the globe and watch the snowfall," he told her. "Here, let me show you."

He took the globe from her hands and shook it until the glittery white flakes were falling over the log cabin, then pointed to the tiny figures of a man and woman standing near a fir tree. "See, that's you and Grandfather when you were young and together."

She smiled and Sawyer didn't miss the lone tear rolling down her wrinkled cheek.

* * *

The next afternoon, after Vivian had helped clear away the huge mess left over from Christmas dinner, she walked down to the horse barn in search of Hannah and Nick and found the children inside the cavernous building, feeding cookies to the stalled horses.

Slipping quietly up behind them, she said in the gruffest voice she could muster, "Okay, you two are caught!"

Both children jumped with fright, then whirled around. Nick's mouth was hanging open, while Hannah's eyes were wide with surprise.

"Oh, Aunt Viv! We're just giving the horses a holiday treat," Nick quickly explained. "Uncle Holt gave us permission. As long as we only feed one cookie to each horse."

Laughing, Vivian hugged an arm around her nephew's shoulders. "I'm only teasing. I'm sure if the horses could talk they'd be saying Merry Christmas."

"What are you doing down here at the barn, Mom?" Hannah asked curiously. "I thought you'd be in the den with everybody else."

Vivian's sly smile included both Hannah and Nick. "I'm going to take a little trip and I thought you two might like to go with me. It's a special Christmas trip," she added.

The cousins shared a look of surprise, then began to jump up and down with eager anticipation.

Hannah was the first to ask, "Right now? Where?"

"Do we have to dress up?" Nick wanted to know. "Did my parents say I could go, too?"

Vivian held up a hand to quieten them. "Yes, Nick, your parents have already okayed it with me. And there's no need for either of you to change clothes. I'm going to visit Sawyer and his grandmother on the Camp Verde reservation. I thought we'd take them some food and gifts."

"We're going to see Sawyer? Yippee!" Hannah shouted

gleefully and grabbed her mother by the arm. "Let's go! We can finish giving cookies to the horses tomorrow. Right, Nick?"

"Right!" Nick soundly agreed. "I've never been to a reservation before. And I want to see Sawyer again. He's a really neat guy."

Vivian smiled at her nephew as the three of them started out of the barn. "You're right, Nick. Sawyer is a neat guy."

He was also the man she'd been waiting on all these years to come into her life, Vivian thought. Yet convincing him that he could be a family man wasn't going to be easy. She could only hope that a bit of Christmas magic would begin to change his way of thinking.

Sawyer was outside, watering the flower garden he'd planted for his grandmother, when he heard a vehicle approaching on the graveled drive that led to the front of the house.

Since the main road branched off before it reached Whitehorse property, there was hardly ever traffic this far back. Most likely one of Nashota's old friends must have decided to drop by to wish her a merry Christmas.

Turning off the hydrant, he put the hose away and turned to see a white truck pulling to a stop in front of the short yard fence. The familiar-looking vehicle caused him to pause. That couldn't be Vivian, could it? She didn't know where he lived. Besides, this was Christmas Day! She was supposed to be with her family.

Walking slowly toward the vehicle, he spotted Vivian stepping down from the driver's side. On the opposite side, Hannah and Nick emerged from the back passenger door.

Both children waved eagerly to him and called out in unison, "Hi, Sawyer! Merry Christmas!"

Lifting an acknowledging hand, he walked through the

gate to meet them, and grinning ear to ear, the youngsters raced over to him.

"Are you surprised to see us?" Hannah asked.

"You three have certainly surprised me," he admitted.

He glanced over to see Vivian had opened the back door on the truck and before Sawyer could ask, Nick said, "Aunt Viv brought some stuff. Maybe we should go help her carry everything."

Sawyer followed the children out to the truck and Vivian promptly turned around and gave him an achingly sweet smile.

"Merry Christmas, Sawyer. I hope you feel like company."

So far today he'd been telling himself how much he was enjoying the quiet. He'd convinced himself that Vivian was right where she belonged, on Three Rivers with her family. But now as he looked at her beautiful, cheery face, he realized how much he'd been missing her.

"Well, since Santa has already come and gone, Grandmother and I could use some company."

"Great!" She reached into the back seat and lifted out a large cardboard box. "You can carry this in for me and I'll let Hannah and Nick carry the gifts."

"You brought gifts?"

Smiling smugly, she placed the box into his outstretched arms. "You didn't think I'd forget you and your grandmother, did you?"

At this moment he wasn't sure what he was thinking. He'd never had a woman visit his home, much less bring gifts on Christmas Day.

"I wasn't expecting to see you today," he admitted. "Isn't your family having a big celebration back at the ranch?"

"Don't worry. They'll still be celebrating tonight. Is your grandmother here? I can't wait to meet her."

"She's in the house. Come along and I'll take you to her."

They headed to the house with the children following behind. When they entered the living room, he said, "Grandmother is probably in the kitchen. We can go in there if you like."

"Sure," Vivian said, then instructed the kids to put the gifts under the tree.

"Oh, this pine is so pretty," Hannah remarked. "Look, Mom, it has tinsel made of real cranberries. That's so cool. We need to make one of these next Christmas."

Nick placed the gift he was carrying alongside the others, but his attention wasn't on the tree, it had already been distracted by a small glass case lying on a nearby table.

"This is really cool, too!" he exclaimed. "Look, Hannah! Here's a bunch of real arrowheads!"

Hannah joined her cousin and immediately gushed over the collections. "Gosh, ours aren't nearly this good. We're going to have to go back to Apache Cove and hunt for more."

Vivian explained to Sawyer. "Hannah and Nick found several arrowheads at Lake Pleasant."

He frowned thoughtfully. "I don't recall seeing that name on the park map. It must be a spot I've never been to."

Vivian shook her head. "It's a secluded area on the shoreline of the lake. And the place doesn't have a real name. Apache Cove is just what I named it."

He smiled at her. "You named it for me and just didn't know it."

Her green eyes twinkled with promises. "I'll take you there. It's...very private," she added in a voice only he could hear.

"I'll hold you to that promise," he said, then taking her by the arm, urged her toward an open doorway.

She called to the children and Sawyer led the four of them across a short hallway to the kitchen. When they entered another open doorway, his grandmother was making coffee in a blue granite pot on the stove.

Sawyer expected Nashota to be very surprised at the sight of Vivian and the children. Instead, the smile on her face implied she'd been expecting them.

He placed the box on the small kitchen table. "Grandmother, we have company. This is Vivian and her daughter, Hannah, and her nephew Nick."

Vivian went straight to Nashota and reached for both her hands. "Hello, Mrs. Whitehorse. I hope you don't mind us showing up without warning," she told her. "I've been wanting to meet you and I didn't want to wait around until Sawyer invited me."

Nashota cast a reproving glance at Sawyer, then nodded at Vivian. "Call me Nashota. And I'm very glad you're here. You and the children."

"Thank you for being so gracious," Vivian told her.

To Sawyer's utter amazement, his grandmother reached up and lovingly framed Vivian's face. "You're very beautiful. And I knew you would come on this Christmas Day."

How could his grandmother have possibly known such a thing? He hadn't known it himself. And why was she treating Vivian as though she'd known her and loved her for years? That wasn't like Nashota. His grandmother had always been careful about who she allowed into her home and her life.

Vivian kissed Nashota's cheek, then motioned for the children to come forward and join them. "You two come say hello to Nashota."

The children politely greeted her with handshakes.

"We brought all kinds of good things to eat," Hannah told her. "Mom made some of her special pumpkin bread. It's yummy."

"My mom is kinda sick," Nick explained to Nashota. "She can hardly eat. She's going to have twins!"

"You're a lucky boy." Nashota patted Nick's shoulder before leveling another pointed look at Sawyer. "Maybe Sawyer will give me twin great-grandchildren someday."

Sawyer cleared his throat. "Why don't we see what's in this food box? I'm hungry."

"Me, too," Nick declared. "I want a piece of toffee."

"Not me. I want ham," Hannah said.

He began to pull out the covered dishes and the five of them gathered around the table.

Nashota poured coffee for the adults and found sodas for the children. After everyone enjoyed the little impromptu meal, they migrated to the living room where Nashota took a seat in her rocker and Sawyer and Vivian shared the couch.

Hannah and Nick played Santa and handed out the gifts. Two to Nashota and one to Sawyer.

"Open yours first, Nashota," Vivian encouraged her, while giving Sawyer a wink. "I'm anxious to see if you like them."

Sawyer watched his grandmother deal with the beautifully wrapped packages while wondering what she could possibly be thinking. Most always she was quiet and guarded around people she'd just met, but today she seemed relaxed and totally enjoying herself.

But when she pulled a cream-colored crocheted shawl from a long flat box, he could see that she was overwhelmed with emotions.

Leaving the couch, he went to her and gently draped the

garment over her shoulders. "You look beautiful, Grandmother. Like a Christmas flower."

She laughed softly. "A faded one, my grandson."

The next gift was a sewing basket filled with all sorts of notions, including a few skeins of bright red yarn.

After Nashota expressed her delight over both gifts, Nick gestured to Sawyer's. "Open yours, Sawyer. Hannah and I helped Vivian pick it out."

Returning to his seat next to Vivian, he picked up the little square box and quickly tore into it. "I wasn't expecting a gift," he said, while tossing the paper aside. "I'm not sure I deserve it."

"Why not?" Hannah piped up. "Grandma says even naughty folks deserve gifts. Cause all of us are naughty at times."

Everyone in the room laughed at that, including his grandmother. "Maureen is obviously a wise woman," he said.

The gift turned out to be a Western-style leather belt tooled in an oak leaf and acorn pattern and buck stitched on both edges. He didn't have to ask to know that the piece had cost Vivian a pretty penny.

"Okay, Sawyer, it's your turn. Do you like your gift?" Vivian asked playfully.

Why was a lump of emotion suddenly choking him? Why was this whole visit from Vivian and the children turning him into a softhearted, sentimental sap? Why was he letting it?

He cleared the tightness in his throat and hoped the questions in his mind would leave with it. "Very much. And it's just my size. How did you guess?"

Her smile was cagey. "I have my ways."

As he thanked her and the children for the gift, Nashota rose from the rocker.

"Would you two kids like to go outside with me? The hens should've laid by now. You can help me gather the eggs."

Nick looked blankly at Hannah, then back to Nashota. "Gosh, you have chickens?"

The boy's surprised reaction clearly amused Nashota. "I sure do. You don't have chickens?"

"No. We only have horses and cows and bulls," Hannah said.

"And dogs and cats," Nick added.

"I see," Nashota said and motioned for the children to follow her. "Well, come with me and I'll teach you about chickens and show you how to gather the eggs."

The three of them left the house and Vivian smiled impishly at him.

"I think your grandmother is trying to give us a few quiet moments together. She's a very special woman, Sawyer. I love her already."

He reached for her hand and pressed it between the two of his. "Trust me, Viv, my grandmother is not that much of a social person. She's never cared much for entertaining. But I can tell she's thrilled about you three being here today. And don't ask me why. I honestly don't know why she's taken to you and the kids."

She leaned close enough to cause her shoulder to press into his and it was all Sawyer could do not to pull her into his arms and place a ravaging kiss on her lips.

"Oh, that's easy to answer, Sawyer. She can see that we truly care about her grandson."

Care? Was this her way of saying love? No! She didn't love him. If she thought she did, then she was as confused and misguided as she'd been back when she'd married her ex, he thought grimly.

"Maybe so. I will say that it's hard to fool Grandmother

about anything." He pushed himself up from the couch. "Stay right there. I'll be back in a minute."

He went to his bedroom and collected a small wrapped package from a chest of drawers, then carried it back to the sofa.

"I didn't expect to see you today to give you your gift. I was going to give it to you tomorrow at work." He handed her the box. "Merry Christmas, Viv."

Totally surprised, her gaze swept from his face to the gift and back to his face. "I don't know what to say, Sawyer. Except that you shouldn't have."

"I shouldn't do a lot of things that I do," he said softly. "But like your mother told Hannah, we're all naughty at one time or another."

She ripped into the package and found the necklace he'd bought at the Western store a few minutes after Hannah had purchased the earrings.

"Oh! Oh, my! It matches my little doves! How beautiful!"

Before he could guess her intentions, she was smacking kisses on the side of his face and the happy reaction put a broad grin on his lips.

"Thank you, Sawyer. You've made this Christmas so special for me. I hope you know that."

He turned his head just enough to bring his lips next to hers. "And I hope you know that you've made my Christmas one I'll never forget."

Or ever experience again.

The thought settled in his heart like a dark, heavy cloud.

Chapter Thirteen

By Friday evening, three days after Vivian had surprised Sawyer and Nashota with the visit on Christmas Day, she realized that something was wrong. Somewhere between that magical day and today some sort of change had come over Sawyer, and she couldn't understand why, or what, if anything, she might've done to cause it.

Now, as she watched him drive away from the headquarters parking lot, she felt worse than deflated. When she'd suggested they make a date to spend time together this weekend, he'd made excuses about needing to finish homework for his online classes. Homework? She'd wanted to point out that most colleges were on recess until the first of the year. But she'd bit her tongue and kept the comment to herself.

Trying to shake away the feeling that Sawyer was deliberately avoiding her, she started to climb into her truck to leave, when she spotted Zane walking across the parking lot toward his vehicle.

With sudden decision, she paused and waved to get his attention. Seeing her, he immediately changed direction and walked over to her.

"Hey, Viv, having trouble with your truck? I can give you a jump if you need it."

She felt her cheeks turning pink. "Thanks, Zane, the truck is fine. I— Actually, I feel like a fool for bothering you. But I—I'm worried about Sawyer. I don't know what's happened to him. Ever since we've come back from Christmas break, he's been—well, distant. I'm not expecting you to talk behind your friend's back. It's just that I'm worried about him."

Zane's gaze dropped sheepishly to the ground and Vivian's heart sunk. These past few days, she'd been patiently biding her time, telling herself that Sawyer's quiet behavior was just an aftereffect of the busy holidays. Now she was beginning to see that she'd only been fooling herself.

"You're right. I don't want to talk about Sawyer behind his back." His expression grim, he lifted his gaze back to her. "But for his own good I think I should."

"What does that mean?"

"He's messed up, Viv. And I tried to tell him so, but he's so damned bullheaded I can't make sense with him."

"It's something about me, isn't it?" she asked with sick certainty. "He—uh—doesn't want to be my partner anymore."

Zane shook his head. "Don't worry. You don't have to hide anything with me, Viv. I've known for a while that you two had a relationship going on. And frankly, I wondered how long Sawyer would allow it to last. Believe me, you've lasted far longer than most."

Vivian wasn't going to shed a tear in front of this man. No, she was far too angry for that.

"So now he's wanting out," she said flatly.

He shrugged one shoulder. "He's asked Mort for a transfer.

I don't have any idea what he told the man. All I know is that Mort promised to deal with the matter in the next few days."

A transfer! Breaking up with her romantically was one thing, but to end their working relationship was really taking things a step above and beyond.

Blowing out a heavy breath, she said, "Thanks, Zane. I'll see you later."

She opened the truck door, while Zane cursed under his breath. "What are you going to do?"

"I'm going to give the man exactly what he wants! That's what I'm going to do!"

She jumped into the truck and, with Zane staring after her, sped out of the parking lot. Once she was on the highway, she pulled her phone from her handbag and punched Sawyer's number.

To her relief he answered after the first ring.

"I don't know where you are on the highway right now, but wherever it is, pull over and stop," she ordered in a seething voice. "I'll be there in five minutes!"

"Viv—what—"

She didn't bother to let him speak. He'd had three days to talk and he'd chosen not to.

Jabbing her finger on the end button, she tossed the phone toward her purse and pressed down hard on the accelerator.

Three minutes later, she spotted his truck parked at a wide pullout near a highway junction. Gravel spewed from her tires when she skidded her vehicle to a stop a few feet away from his.

"What the hell are you doing?" he demanded, as they met at a spot between the two trucks. "Trying to kill yourself?"

"Not hardly. I wouldn't want to make things that easy for you," she said with enough sarcasm to cause his eyebrows to arch in disbelief.

Hanging his thumbs over his belt, he rocked back on the heels of his boots. "Okay. What's this about? I could tell by your call that you're angry, but—"

"Angry?" She let out a short, caustic laugh. "That can't begin to describe what I'm feeling right now! And don't waste my time giving me that blank, innocent look. You *know* what this is about."

His nostrils flared as he glanced off to a spot beyond her shoulder. "How did you find out?"

"I pried it out of Zane."

"That damned big-mouth," he muttered.

"Don't be blaming Zane for your behavior."

"He had no right telling you my business!"

Vivian hadn't thought it was possible to get any angrier, but she was. Her breaths were coming at a rapid pace, while her hands were balled into fists so tight that her fingers ached.

"Your business," she said through clenched teeth. "You think it isn't my business, too? I'm supposed to be your partner! You asked for a transfer and you tell me it's none of my business? Go to hell, Sawyer!"

She started to walk away, but he caught her by the arm and tugged her back to him. "Listen, Viv, this is for the best. You need to understand I'm leaving for your sake."

Jerking her arm from his grasp, she glared at him. "Don't feed me any more of your lines, Sawyer. You're nothing but a user. A big coward and a hypocrite to boot! And furthermore, you don't need to bother about getting a transfer. There's zero danger of me putting my hands on you again!"

In the waning light she could see his features growing tight with anger. It was an emotion she'd never seen on him before and the sight left her feeling cold and terribly lost. The Sawyer she'd known and fallen in love with had vanished before her very eyes.

"Don't worry, Vivian. You won't be bothered with seeing me at work or anywhere else. With or without a transfer I'm leaving Lake Pleasant for good!"

He walked off and Vivian didn't wait to see what he did after that. Her heart breaking, she climbed back into her truck and headed it in the direction of Three Rivers.

By the end of the following week, Sawyer pretty much hated himself and it didn't help his frame of mind to have Zane reminding him every few minutes of how much of an idiot he'd been to walk away from Vivian.

Hell, he didn't need his friend or his grandmother to tell him that he'd given up the best thing he'd ever had, or would have in his life. He'd known that long before he'd made the painful decision to part ways with her and Lake Pleasant.

Now, as the two men sat in Burro Crossing, eating burgers and fries, Zane continued to beat the subject of Vivian to death.

"I don't get it," Zane said. "You told me how Christmas Day with Vivian was the best holiday you'd ever had. You said your grandmother couldn't have been happier. Why did you turn around and ruin it all?"

"Zane, I'm beginning to think you have half a brain. And you're not even using a quarter of that part. I had to end things with Vivian. She was—" She was falling in love with him and Sawyer was falling in love with her. As euphoric and wonderful as that had been, he was smart enough to know the feelings couldn't last. Not with a man like him. He didn't know the first thing about being a husband or father. And he'd never be able to give her the life she was accustomed to. "Viv was getting too close and making things...uncomfortable."

Zane studied him for long, thoughtful moments. "Ah,

I see. The same old Sawyer running away from reality. Well, you really fixed things for her. She doesn't have a partner now. Mort can't find a replacement. I volunteered but he wasn't keen on the idea."

"Thank God," Sawyer snarled. "She doesn't need you around to make her life miserable!"

"Hah! We both know who's made her miserable and it sure as hell isn't me."

Sawyer picked up his burger but couldn't bring himself to take a bite. All he could think about was Vivian making rounds through the campsites alone. Hiking the trails alone and dealing with unruly park guests without anyone to back her up. The very idea made him sick and he mentally cursed Mort for not doing something about the situation.

You don't need to be cursing anyone but yourself, Sawyer. You made the choice to end things. You're the one who decided she would be better off without you than with you.

Across the table, Zane shook his head. "Forget it, man. Eat your food. You look like you need it." He took a swig of beer, then leveled a pointed look at Sawyer. "So what are you going to do about work? Return to Dead Horse Ranch?"

"I have plenty of comp time to use. Before it runs out I figure Mort will have me transferred back to Dead Horse. At least, that's what he told me."

"Guess that'll probably be for the best," Zane said shrewdly. "You can go back to your philandering ways and forget all about Viv."

"Yeah. I'll forget all about her. Just like always."

The words tasted like bitter gall, but Sawyer didn't bother to reach for his drink. Nothing could wash away the pain of losing Vivian.

* * *

"Mom, what are you doing sitting out here by yourself?"

Vivian looked up from her seat on the firepit to see Hannah stepping onto the patio. Not wanting her daughter to suspect the misery going on inside her, she purposely straightened her shoulders and plastered a smile on her face.

"Oh, just enjoying the fire that Matt built. Pretty soon the weather will be getting too warm for this."

Hannah took a seat next to her. "Uncle Blake and Aunt Katherine are going to play Monopoly with me and Nick. We thought you'd like to play, too."

"I might join in on the next game. I'm rather tired tonight. With it being Friday, the park was very busy with guests coming in for the weekend."

Hannah shot her a hopeful glance. "Since tomorrow is Saturday that means you and Sawyer don't have to work. Can we go to the reservation to see him and Nashota?"

Only yesterday Hannah had asked when Sawyer was going to visit Three Rivers again and not wanting to disappoint her, Vivian had evaded telling her the truth. How could she explain to her that Sawyer would never be coming back to the ranch, or Lake Pleasant?

Vivian realized she was being cowardly by not telling Hannah the truth of the matter, but it was obvious just how much her daughter had come to love Sawyer in the short amount of time she'd known him. The man had that kind of effect on people, she thought ruefully. He charmed and drew on everyone's affections, without one thought to the grief he might cause later on.

"Not tomorrow," Vivian said, trying to make herself sound as casual as possible. "I'm not sure when we might go."

"Why not? We had a wonderful time. I loved Nashota.

She told me and Nick lots of funny stories about the chickens and the coyotes. And Sawyer is the best." She let out a dreamy sigh. "You know, Mom, I always thought you'd probably never find a boyfriend. And then I was afraid if you did, he'd be a jerk or a nerd. But Sawyer is perfect."

The pain in the middle of Vivian's chest was practically unbearable and she wondered if her heart was actually splitting down the middle.

"No one is perfect, Hannah."

"Well, Sawyer is close to it," she happily pointed out. "He'd make a great dad for me. Just like Uncle Blake did for Nick."

Vivian couldn't bring herself to dampen her daughter's wishes. Not just yet. Maybe in a few days she'd be able to gather her broken emotions enough to be able to talk with Hannah and not dissolve into tears.

"Uh, right now I'm not working with Sawyer," she said, the words barely squeaking past her tight throat. "He had to go to another park."

Hannah appeared stunned and it was all Vivian could do to keep her tears at bay. She'd not been able to give her daughter a responsible, loving father. Now, just as Hannah was beginning to hope that Sawyer was going to step into that role, she'd failed her daughter again. It was time Vivian faced the truth. She was no good with men.

"Another park? For how long?"

"I'm not sure about that. Maybe a long time. He might not ever get to come back to Lake Pleasant."

The crestfallen expression on Hannah's precious face tore the hole in Vivian's heart even deeper.

"Maybe never. Gosh. No wonder you've been so sad here lately."

Vivian attempted to smile. "I'm not sad, honey. And

please don't worry about me. You go on and enjoy your Monopoly game. I'll be there in a few minutes."

Hannah looked as though she wanted to argue, but something must have suddenly changed her mind. Whatever it was, Vivian was grateful. She didn't want to answer any more questions about Sawyer tonight.

"Okay, Mom. You just rest and enjoy the fire."

She kissed Vivian's cheek and hurried back through the French doors.

Ten minutes later, Vivian pushed herself to her feet with intentions of going back into the house, but paused when she saw her brother Holt step onto the patio. For the past three days he'd been gone to a horse auction in California and she'd missed him.

"Hello, brother, when did you get home?"

Smiling, he walked over and gave her shoulders a brief hug. "A couple of hours ago. I missed supper."

"Because you were down at the horse barn trying to figure out where you were going to put all the horses you're having shipped from California. Right?" she asked.

He chuckled. "I could never fool you. Yep, I bought a few. Just ten this time."

"Ten! Holt, you have a disease. You need to be vaccinated for horse-itis."

"There's not such a disease," he said with another chuckle. "Besides, how can I help myself when Blake hands me a blank check and tells me to get what I want?"

"No self-control. That's your problem."

But who was she to talk. If she'd had enough self-control to keep her distance from Sawyer, her heart wouldn't be tearing into aching bits. If she'd kept her ears shut to all his sweet, but phony words, she would've never gone to bed with the man.

Another tragic mistake on her part, she thought sickly.

At least she hadn't gone so far as to marry him like she had Garth. The idea very nearly made her choke with bitter laughter. Marriage with Sawyer? He would've jumped off a cliff at Indian Mesa to keep from marrying her, or any woman.

"I guess Blake doesn't have any self-control, either. Now that he's learned he's going to be the father of twins, he's been in a generous mood."

Holt took a seat in one of the lawn chairs positioned close to the fire ring and motioned for Vivian to sit in the one next to his.

She shook her head. "I told Hannah I'd be inside to play a board game. She's going to think I'm not coming."

"Forget about the game. She and Nick sent me out here to talk to you."

Sighing, Vivian eased into the spare lawn chair. "Okay, what are those two wanting me to do now? If it's another trip to Dragoon, they're just going to have to wait. I'm carrying an extra load at work and—"

He held up a hand to interrupt her. "Whoa! Slow down. This isn't anything like that. Your daughter and nephew are worried about you and they thought I might help fix whatever's wrong." A gentle smile touched his face. "For some reason they seemed to think I can talk to you better than anyone else in the family."

Her brother's concern caused something inside her to break, making it impossible for Vivian to continue to hide her misery. Tears filled her eyes and spilled onto her cheeks. "I'm sorry, Holt. God knows I've tried to keep all this hidden from Hannah. She doesn't deserve to be hurt by my bad judgment. Not again!"

"What are you talking about? Has something happened with you and Sawyer?"

Sniffing back her tears she gave him a quick explanation of everything that had happened since Christmas Day. "I'll be honest, Holt, when I found out he'd asked for a transfer I was totally blindsided. I mean, those few days after Christmas I could see he wasn't quite himself. But I never guessed he had the intentions to end things between us." She looked at him and shook her head. "Your big sister has to be one of the stupidest women in Yavapai County and beyond."

"Why? For falling in love? I wouldn't call that stupid. I'd call it being human. And God knows you haven't allowed yourself to be human in a long time."

"Yeah, well, look what it's done for me," she said in a voice heavy with sarcasm.

"As far as I can see you're still upright and breathing."

She grimaced. "I don't care about me anymore. It's my darling little Hannah that worries me. She wants a father so much. She wants siblings. And when I started dating Sawyer, I could see her getting her hopes up. Now—I just can't bring myself to tell her that Sawyer is out of our lives."

"Damn it, Viv! You're not going to tell her any such thing. You're going to get a grip on yourself and quit being a fraidy-cat. If you really love Sawyer then you need to put your fears behind you and go after him. Grab on to him and don't let go."

Her tears vanished as she stared incredulously at her brother. "Fraidy-cat! Just where do you come off calling me that? And you have no business telling me what to do about my love life. You're the biggest tomcat that's ever prowled the state of Arizona."

He chuckled. "That's a mighty big area. But thank you for the compliment."

"You're insufferable! And you make me furious! And I—" The cocky smile on his face doused her anger and suddenly she was laughing and sobbing at the same time. "I love you, Holt."

He drew her up from the chair and hugged her. "Of course you do. And you love Sawyer, too. I could see that even before he came to visit Three Rivers. Don't pass this chance by, my sister. Or you'll regret it from now on."

Holt was right. She truly did love Sawyer. And if she didn't fight for him now, she might as well tattoo the word *coward* across her forehead and cry away the rest of her life.

She kissed her brother's cheek. "Thank you, Holt. Let's go in and see if there's any of Reeva's coconut cake left. If I'm going to put my fighting gloves on tomorrow I'm going to need my strength."

He laughed. "Now you're talking, sister!"

The next morning, Sawyer was up early, hammering steeples into the fence posts surrounding his grandmother's chicken house, when he caught the sound of Nashota's voice behind him.

"I think you've driven enough steeples to hold that wire in place for the next ten years."

Lowering the hammer, he turned around to see she was dressed for going out. "I don't want it to sag. If a coyote sees a space he can get through, he'll take it. Then you won't have a hen left."

Moving closer, she frowned at him. "You're going overboard with precautions, Sawyer. When are you going to start trusting yourself?"

Trusting himself? What did that have to do with keeping these damned laying hens safe from coyotes?

The morning was unusually warm for January, causing sweat to collect on his forehead. He used the forearm of his sleeve to wipe it away before he said, "I want things protected."

"Yes," she said sagely. "Especially your feelings. I've always known that."

Bemused by her offhand remarks, he shook his head. "What are you doing dressed like that? Are you and Anita going to town?"

She clasped her hands together. "No. Anita has gone to Flagstaff to see her daughter. You're going to take me."

Other than the monthly market at Camp Verde where she sold the jewelry she crafted, his grandmother rarely went anywhere. And he knew for a fact that the market wasn't going on this weekend.

"I am, am I? Where to? The grocery store?"

"No. We're going to Three Rivers Ranch. That is where Vivian and her daughter live."

If Sawyer hadn't been leaning against the cedar fence post, he would have fallen face forward. "Grandmother, what in the hell has come over you? We're not going to Three Rivers! And that's that!"

The look she gave him made Sawyer glad she didn't have a hoe or rake in her hand. Otherwise she would've been flogging him with the wooden handle.

"You have never told me no before," she said flatly. "And you are not about to start now. Go change your clothes. We're going."

Frustration swamped him, yet he did his best to hold on to his temper. "You don't understand, Grandmother! Viv and I aren't seeing each other anymore. That's why I transferred away from Lake Pleasant. So I wouldn't have to see her. I don't want to go to Three Rivers and be humiliated all over again."

"I know why you aren't at Lake Pleasant. And I know why you ran away from Vivian."

He didn't know where or how his grandmother got her information. She rarely used the phone and she didn't often question him about his personal life. Yet somehow she seemed to know these things about him without him saying a word.

He let out a cynical grunt. "I don't call it running away. I call it using good sense."

Ignoring that, she said, "For years you've believed you would end up like your father—hurt by an unhappy woman. I've never tried to change your mind because I could see the women you dated were not important to you. Now you're in love and I can see you are hurting. The pain won't go away until you show Vivian what's really in your heart."

He studied his grandmother's wise face as her advice circled around in his tortured thoughts. The pain inside him wouldn't go away, he conceded. Not unless he had Vivian back in his arms.

"Vivian is from a wealthy family. She has everything she wants or needs."

"She doesn't have you."

Sawyer groaned as he felt his resistance crumbling like a piece of old adobe.

"All right, Grandmother. I'll take you to Three Rivers. But don't be embarrassed when Vivian orders me off the place."

"When you get as old as I am, Sawyer, you don't get embarrassed."

Sawyer tossed the hammer he'd been holding into a wooden toolbox, then reached for his grandmother's arm.

"We'd better get started. It's a long way from here to Three Rivers."

In more ways than one, he thought ruefully. But could Nashota be right? Could Vivian want him just as much or more than everything she had at Three Rivers? He'd soon find out.

Chapter Fourteen

Vivian glimpsed at her image in the vanity mirror one last time. A pair of skinny jeans, cowboy boots and a bright yellow sweater wasn't exactly a romantic outfit or one that shouted seduction. But this trip to the reservation to see Sawyer wasn't about luring him to his uncle's old house for a romp in the bed.

She had to use this opportunity to convince him that she truly cared about him. She had to make him realize they were meant to be together and that nothing about their pasts, or age difference, or the money in their bank accounts should stand between them.

With a determined glint in her eye, she turned away from the mirror and grabbed her handbag and jacket off the bed.

She was halfway down the staircase when her mother appeared at the bottom step.

"Viv, are you ready to leave?"

Vivian paused. "Yes. Why? The kids aren't whining to go with me, are they?"

"Oh, no. They both understand you need to be alone when you see Sawyer today. In fact, they've already left with Matt to go gather cattle."

Vivian breathed a sigh of relief as she descended the remaining stairs to join her mother. "That's great. So was there something else?"

"I know you're in a hurry to leave, but I need a favor—if you don't mind."

Vivian couldn't believe her mother was doing this. "What is it?"

She held up a manila envelope. "Blake is already at his office to meet a cattle buyer and he needs these registration papers so they can be attached to the transfers. Can you run them down to the ranch yard for me?"

Vivian frowned while thinking this whole favor of hers sounded contrived. Blake never forgot things he needed, and if he did, he'd walk back to the house to fetch them himself.

"I suppose I can take them."

Maureen handed her the envelope. "I realize you're in a bit of a hurry and I'd do it myself, but my knee is giving me fits. I twisted it yesterday when I was climbing out of the saddle."

Vivian's skepticism grew. Less than thirty minutes ago, she'd seen her mother racing through the kitchen with the spryness of a twenty-year-old. Obviously Maureen was trying to detain her for some reason. A fact that hardly made sense, but she wasn't going to waste more time pressing her mother on the matter.

"Don't worry, Mom. I'll get them right to him and then I'll leave." She leaned over and kissed her mother's cheek. "Wish me luck."

"I wish you all the luck in the world, darling. Drive safely."

Vivian dashed away and walked in record time to Blake's office. The cattle buyer had already arrived and with the two men in deep discussion, she discreetly placed the envelope on the corner of her brother's desk and made a quick exit.

She was halfway back to the front of the house when she spotted a pickup truck rounding the circular drive. Most all the visitors who had business dealings with the ranch drove straight to the ranch yard rather than stop in front of the house. Which made her suspect her mother was about to receive company.

Hurrying forward, her thoughts strayed to Sawyer and exactly what she was going to say to him. She didn't expect anything about seeing him again to be easy. No. She figured his initial reaction would be to tell her to get lost. But she wasn't going to let that put her off. Her love for him was too deep, too precious to simply toss away as though it could be easily replaced. Nothing about her feelings for Sawyer could ever be replaced.

She was almost to her vehicle when she caught a glimpse of her mother walking across the front porch and down the steps. Without the slightest hitch in her knee, Vivian thought wryly.

Curious, her gaze strayed to the truck that had parked near the front gate and suddenly she stopped dead in her tracks.

It was Sawyer! And Nashota was with him! What were they doing here?

Her heart suddenly hammering out of control, she moved slowly forward until she was standing a few feet away from where her mother was welcoming Nashota with a hug.

Was this why Maureen had been trying to detain her?

Because she knew Sawyer and his grandmother were coming? But why? How?

Her mind whirling with questions and a faint ray of hope, she forced herself to join them.

"There you are," Maureen said, acknowledging Vivian's arrival. "As you can see we have company."

She darted a wary glance at Sawyer before gathering Nashota in a gentle hug.

"Hello, Nashota," she said. "It's wonderful to see you again."

She patted Vivian's cheek. "I'm happy to see you again, too."

Before anything else could be said, Maureen took the older woman by the arm. "Let's go inside, Nashota, and leave these two to talk."

Stunned by this turn of events, Vivian watched the two women disappear into the house before she turned back to Sawyer. His expression was stoic, almost like he was numb. Vivian couldn't blame him. Not when she felt just as numb.

"I don't understand, Sawyer. What are you doing here?"

He glanced in the direction of the house. "I think I've been manipulated by a pair of women."

Her heart sank. "Oh. I thought—" She broke off as all the words she'd been rehearsing in her mind flew away with the wind.

A pained look came over his face. "Thought what? That I should know better than to return to Three Rivers?"

Seeing that his thinking was still way off track, she stepped closer, while trying to collect her scattered senses. "No. Actually, I was about to climb into my truck to head to your house. But I think— Mom must have known you were coming. She sent me off on a useless errand to detain me."

A look of disbelief washed over his face. "You were coming to my house? Why?"

She groaned as her composure began to break. "To... try to make you understand that I...don't want to go on without you in my life, Sawyer."

His brown eyes studied her for long, tense moments and then with a needy groan, his hands reached for her shoulders. She stumbled into his arms and buried the side of her face into the middle of his chest.

"Viv! I thought— I never expected you to want to see me again!"

"I know that's what you wanted. That's what you had planned when you asked Mort for the transfer, but—"

"You were right, Viv, when you called me a coward and a user. That's exactly what I've been for all my adult years." His arms tightened around her. "When I met you I believed everything would be fun and games with us. Just like it had always been with me. But something crazy happened to me along the way. I fell in love with you. And it scared the hell out of me. On Christmas Day—"

"I thought you were happy that day," she interrupted. "I thought it felt as magical to you as it did to me. And then the next day at work I could feel something was wrong."

With a thumb beneath her chin, he tilted her face up to his.

"That was me running scared, Viv. And to be honest, I'm still scared. I don't know anything about being a husband or father. All I know about marriage is that it made my parents miserable. But I had to come see you this morning, anyway. Because I love you. Because somehow I want us to try to fit our lives together. Not just for a while but for always."

Her heart spilling over with love, she cupped her hands around his dear, familiar face. "I love you, too, Sawyer. So very much. And you weren't the only one of us who was frightened. All I could think was that I was falling for a man who didn't need a woman who was six years older than him. Especially one with a daughter nearing her teenage years."

He smiled and the sight of it chased away all the doubts and fears that tormented her this past week without him.

"Those six extra years look mighty beautiful on you, Viv. And as for Hannah, I'm going to try my best to be the father she deserves. And a good father to the other children we'll hopefully be blessed with."

Happy tears filled her eyes. "How did this happen? You never intended to be a family man."

"This past week and a half without you has shown me that being a family man is the only thing I'll ever want to be."

Laughing, she pulled his head down so that she could give his lips a long, lingering kiss.

When it finally ended, she said, "You know, when Nashota told you the job at Lake Pleasant was going to bring you great fortune, she was actually wrong. It brought the great fortune to me."

"No, my darling. To the both of us."

The smile on her face came from deep within her heart. "Yes, to the both of us," she agreed, then slipping an arm across the back of his waist, she urged him toward the house.

Epilogue

Six months later on a hot July evening, the Hollisters were not only celebrating Independence Day, but also the birth of Katherine and Blake's twins. Three nights ago, Andrew and Abigail had arrived right on schedule and since then, Blake had been practically guarding the door of the nursery to make sure the babies weren't disturbed by his big, doting family.

As for Vivian and Sawyer, they'd gotten married back in January in the little church on the reservation where Sawyer had attended services since he was a small boy. The ceremony had been simple, but especially lovely with the nave and sanctuary decorated with sunflowers, a symbol of happiness for Apaches. After they'd spoken their vows, the minister had prayed the Apache wedding prayer and in that moment, as the beautiful words had poured over her, Vivian had no doubt that she was with the right man. And he would love her for the rest of their lives.

After the wedding, she and Sawyer had managed to get a few days off from work to spend a quiet honeymoon in Flagstaff. Once it was over, she and Hannah had moved in with Sawyer and Nashota in their little house on the Camp Verde reservation.

At first Vivian had been worried her daughter might resist moving away from Nick and the horses, but surprisingly she'd been all for the idea. Since then, Sawyer had built a barn and corral large enough for Hannah to keep two horses and with Nick being a frequent visitor, Hannah seemed more than content with her new home. She had a father now, whom she loved dearly.

"What are you doing sitting here by yourself?" Sawyer asked as he joined her beneath the shade of a cottonwood tree. "Holt says the homemade ice cream is almost ready."

Vivian laughed. "You can't trust what he says. He's too impatient to wait until it's completely frozen."

Sawyer surveyed the crowd of family and friends bunched around the patio. "Take a look over there. In the glider," he said, pointing a discreet finger at an area of lawn behind the patio. "Grandmother and Sam are really hitting it off. Who would've thought?"

Vivian eyed the old couple, who were sitting with their heads together, talking up a storm. "I hope he hasn't offered her any whiskey yet," Vivian said with a chuckle.

Rising from the lawn chair, she reached for her husband's hand and squeezed his fingers. "Are you having a good time?"

"I always have a super time when I'm with your family. To be honest, I'm still in shock that Mort gave both of us the day off. The park is running over with guests. And it's taking every ranger on the roster to make sure no firecrackers are set off to create wildfires."

So far Vivian and Sawyer were still working together at Lake Pleasant. To their surprise and delight, Mort had secretly torn up Sawyer's request for a transfer. However, Sawyer had recently finished his college studies and was considering the management job at Dead Horse Ranch Park.

Vivian loved working with her husband, yet she understood the promotion was something he'd been working toward long before the two of them had met. She recognized the importance he placed on acquiring a better position with a higher salary. As a man he needed to feel that he contributed just as much or more to their family unit as she did. Vivian realized to some women that way of thinking might seem old-fashioned, but it seemed perfectly wonderful to her. Having him love and protect and provide for her made her feel more like a woman than she'd ever felt in her life.

"Hey, Mom, Dad! Come on! We're dishing up the ice cream!"

Vivian looked across the yard to see Hannah waving to catch their attention.

Sawyer chuckled. "Sounds like we're wanted for a good cause."

A short time later, Vivian and Sawyer were sitting with Joseph and Tessa and enjoying the frozen dessert, when Maureen strolled by the table and paused to rest her hands on Sawyer's shoulders.

"Have you two seen the twins yet?" she asked, directing the question to her son-in-law and daughter.

Vivian laughed. "Barely. With papa bear Blake guarding them like Fort Knox."

Sawyer said, "They're a fine pair. I thought Andrew resembled Blake. But with all that brown hair Abigail is a mirror image of her brother Nick."

"I hope the twins gave you some ideas," Maureen suggested slyly. "Vivian isn't getting any younger, you know."

Vivian let out a playful shriek. "Mom! That's an awful thing to say about me!"

Joseph turned a loving look on his wife. "The new babies have certainly given Tessa all sorts of ideas. But then, she already had plenty of those before the two tots arrived."

Tessa pulled a playful face at her husband. "You don't think we're going to let little Joseph grow up without siblings, do you?"

He leaned over and kissed her cheek. "Not hardly."

Sawyer glanced up at his mother-in-law. "Don't worry, Maureen. I'm making plans to add a room onto the house for a nursery. If I have anything to say about it, you'll have several more grandchildren to spoil."

Maureen gave him an approving wink, then moved away to mingle with the rest of the crowd.

The moment she was out of earshot, Joseph leaned across the table and spoke in a hushed voice. "Viv, something strange is going on with Mom."

"Reeva said basically the same thing to me six months ago," Vivian told him. "Since then I've tried to urge Mom to spill what's on her mind, but she insists there's nothing wrong."

Frowning, Joseph shook his head. "She's covering up something."

Vivian and Sawyer exchanged concerned glances.

"What makes you think that?" Vivian asked her brother.

"Earlier this evening, when we were in the study, she told me and Blake that she's weary of dwelling on the cause of Dad's death. She says as far as she's concerned she's closing the door on the idea that the incident was more than an accident."

Stunned, Vivian shook her head. "That can't be! Mom has always wanted to uncover the actual cause of Dad's death. Something has caused her to change her mind. But what?"

"I wish we had the answer, sis. It might help us get to the truth of the matter."

Later that night, as Sawyer and Vivian sat on a bale of hay and watched fireworks dance across the starlit sky, he pulled her close to his side.

"You're not still worrying about your mother, are you?"

With a wan smile, she shook her head. "No. Mom is a very strong woman, but this thing about Dad has hung over her for several years now. I think she just wants to be free of the sadness. To close that chapter of her life and move forward. I can't blame her for that. You and I have done the same thing and look how happy it's made us."

He kissed her lips, then nuzzled a spot close to her ear. "I always wanted a woman who'd give me plenty of fireworks. You've given me those and a whole lot more, my beautiful wife. I have to be the happiest man on earth."

Smiling, she asked, "Were you serious about building an extra room for a nursery?"

His eyes full of love, he traced a finger over her cheek. "Absolutely. Think you're ready to be a mother again?"

She turned her head just enough to press her lips to his cheek. "With my trusty ranger by my side, I'm ready for anything."

* * * * *

*If you loved this story, be sure to check out
Stella Bagwell's next book, part of the
Fortunes of Texas: The Lost Fortunes continuity,
coming in April 2019!*

*And for more in the
Men of the West miniseries,
try these books, available now from
Harlequin Special Edition:*

Her Man on Three Rivers Ranch
The Arizona Lawman
Her Kind of Doctor
The Cowboy's Christmas Lullaby

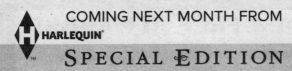

"Lisa," the man dressed as Zorro said, "I'd heard you were going to be here."

He clearly thought Julie was someone else. She probably ought to say something, but up close, the gorgeous bandito seemed to have stolen both her thoughts and her words.

"It's nice to finally meet you." His deep voice set her senses reeling. "I've never really liked blind dates."

Talk about masquerades and mistaken identities. Before Julie could set him straight, he took her hand in a polished, gentlemanly manner and kissed it. His warm breath lingered on her skin, setting off a bevy of butterflies in her tummy.

"Dance with me," he said.

Her lips parted, but for the life of her, she still couldn't speak, couldn't explain. And she darn sure couldn't object.

Zorro led her away from the buffet tables and to the dance floor. When he opened his arms, she again had the opportunity to tell him who she really was. But instead, she stepped into his embrace, allowing him to take the lead.

His alluring aftershave, something manly, taunted her. As she savored his scent, as well as the warmth of his muscular arms, her pulse soared. She leaned her head on his shoulder as they swayed to a sensual beat, their movements in perfect accord, as though they'd danced together a hundred times before.

Now would be a good time to tell him she wasn't Lisa, but she seemed to have fallen under a spell that grew stronger with every beat of the music. The moment turned surreal, like she'd stepped into a fairy tale with a handsome rogue.

Once again, she pondered revealing his mistake and telling him her name, but there'd be time enough to do that after the song ended. Then she'd return to the kitchen, slipping off like Cinderella. But instead of a glass slipper, she'd leave behind her momentary enchantment.

But several beats later, a cowboy tapped Zorro on the shoulder. "I need you to come outside."

Zorro looked at him and frowned. "Can't you see I'm busy?"

The cowboy, whose outfit was so authentic he seemed to be the real deal, rolled his eyes.

Julie wished she could have worn her street clothes. Would now be a good time to admit that she wasn't an actual attendee but here to work at the gala?

"What's up?" Zorro asked.

The cowboy folded his arms across his chest and shifted his weight to one hip. "Someone just broke into my pickup."

Zorro's gaze returned to Julie. "I'm sorry, Lisa. I'm going to have to morph into cop mode."

Now it was Julie's turn to tense. He was actually a police officer in real life? A slight uneasiness settled over her, an old habit she apparently hadn't outgrown. Not that she had any real reason to fear anyone in law enforcement nowadays.

Don't miss
The Lawman's Convenient Family *by Judy Duarte,*
available January 2019 wherever
Harlequin® Special Edition books and ebooks are sold.

www.Harlequin.com

#1 *New York Times* bestselling author

LINDA LAEL MILLER

presents:

**The next great contemporary read from
Harlequin Special Edition author Judy Duarte!
A touching story about the magic of creating a
family and developing romantic relationships.**

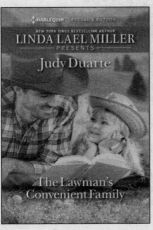

*"Will you marry me, for a
while?"*

Adam Santiago's always
been a lone ranger. But
when the detective teams
up with music therapist
Julie Chapman to save
two young orphans, pretty
soon *his* heart's a goner,
too! Julie's willing to do
anything—even become
Adam's pretend bride—to
keep a brother and sister
together. But as she falls
head over heels for her polar opposite, will this marriage
of convenience become an affair of the heart?

**Available December 18,
wherever books are sold.**

Looking for more satisfying love stories
with community and family at their core?

Check out **Harlequin® Special Edition**
and **Love Inspired®** books!

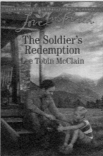

New books available every month!

CONNECT WITH US AT:

Facebook.com/groups/HarlequinConnection

 Facebook.com/HarlequinBooks

 Twitter.com/HarlequinBooks

 Instagram.com/HarlequinBooks

 Pinterest.com/HarlequinBooks

ReaderService.com

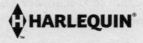

**ROMANCE WHEN
YOU NEED IT**

HFGENRE2018